H. G. PARRY

This special signed edition is limited to 1000 numbered copies.

This is copy 74.

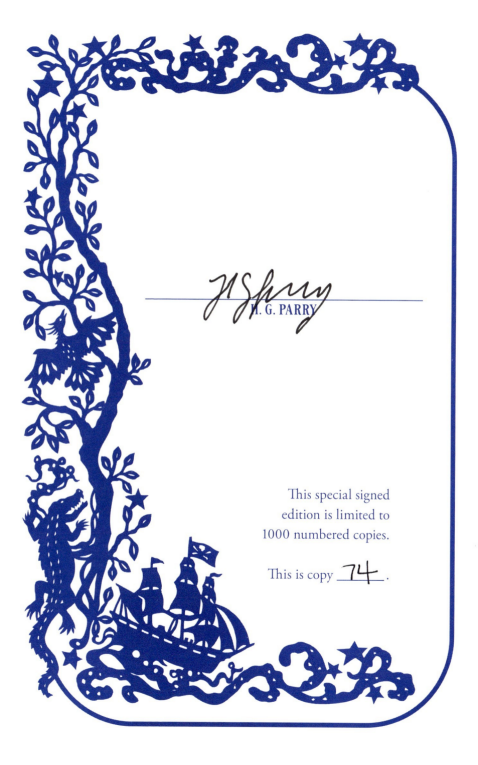

HEARTLESS

Heartless
H. G. Parry

SUBTERRANEAN PRESS 2024

Heartless
Copyright © 2024 by H. G. Parry.
All rights reserved.

Dust jacket and interior illustrations
Copyright © 2024 by Kathleen Jennings.
All rights reserved.

Interior design
Copyright © 2024 by Desert Isle Design, LLC.
All rights reserved.

Edited by Navah Wolfe

First Edition

ISBN
978-1-64524-164-5

Subterranean Press
PO Box 190106
Burton, MI 48519

subterraneanpress.com

Manufactured in the United States of America

*Sometimes, though not often, [Peter] had dreams,
and they were more painful than the dreams of other
boys. For hours he could not be separated from
these dreams, though he wailed piteously in them.
They had to do, I think, with the riddle of his existence.*

—*Peter Pan*, Chapter 13, "Do You Believe in Fairies?"

I

Peter Breaks Through

JAMES didn't know about Peter's heart when he met him, just after midnight on his first night in the workhouse. Peter was ten, or so it was rumoured. James was seven, and his mother had just died. He hadn't cried then; nor had he cried when they buried her in the cold earth beneath a pauper's grave; nor when he had been pushed through the great doors in the workhouse courtyard, scoured clean, dressed in thin gray cloth, and set alongside so many other boys his age. His mother had always told him to never let them see him cry. He was a gentleman, she said, like his father had been, and a gentleman never cries. But it was dark in the boys' dormitory, and nobody was looking. He lay beneath his blanket, raw and empty, the sobs he had fought all day coming in sharp, jagged bursts. He thought the rest of the room was asleep until the voice came.

"Why are you crying?" it said.

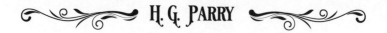

James sat up with a sniffle, grief dulled by surprise. A boy sat cross-legged at the foot of his bed. The boy was as fair and strong as James was dark and slight; in the moonlight, his small white teeth gleamed. For a moment, James could only think that a spirit had flown in through the window.

"Who—who are you?" he asked.

"Peter," the boy said, which wasn't a usual name for a spirit. "I've lived here longer than anyone—since I was a week old. You're the new boy. Why are you crying?"

James, who was indeed the new boy, considered his answer carefully. It wasn't that he didn't know—of course he did. It was just so obvious that he didn't know how to put it into words.

"I miss my mother," he said at last. "And I want to go home."

"I don't have a home," Peter said. "I ran away the day I was born. I didn't want to grow up."

This was very strange; strange enough to distract James from his misery. He himself longed to grow up. Everybody he knew did. The only children who didn't grow up were the ones sleeping under the wooden crosses in the paupers' graveyard.

"Y—you left your family behind?" he ventured.

Peter shrugged, careless.

"But what about your mother?"

"I don't have a mother," Peter said.

James knew then, with a sense of awe, that he was in the presence of a tragedy. The tragedy was not that Peter did not have a mother: many of the children in that terrible room did not. The tragedy was that Peter didn't care. It gave him an indefinable glamour, while James, like the other children, was

merely a lost, dirty scrap of humanity who cried at night when nobody was listening.

The two boys looked at each other in the moonlight, wary and fascinated as two animals meeting in a clearing. Peter saw the tears on James's face. James saw the lack of them on Peter's.

Peter's interest waned first. As James would find later, it always did. Yet something of it must have remained, because he leaned forward instead of turning away. That was the first time James noticed the puzzling thing about Peter's heart. It was louder than most hearts—he could hear the beat of it across the quiet space between them. But it didn't sound like a heartbeat. It had the low, resonant tick-tock of a clock.

"I suppose *you* had a mother," Peter said. "Did she tell you any stories?"

"Oh, yes." He thought, suddenly, that he might cry again after all. "Every night."

"Bet you can't remember them."

"I can!" James protested. "I remember every word."

Peter stretched, and leaned back on his elbows expectantly. "Go on then," he said.

EVEN AFTER he had been accepted by the inmates of the workhouse as Peter's friend, James knew that he wouldn't have stayed Peter's friend for very long had it not been for the stories. Peter was notoriously fickle. He took fancies to newcomers all the time; the next day, he would not even remember their names. Once, shortly after James had arrived,

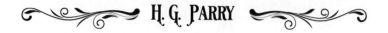

he had seen Peter give a new boy the pan flute that had been a present from James himself. James had made it, whittling it piece by piece from bits of wood over six long months as an old sailor who used to visit his mother had once taught him. The betrayal hurt him deeply, until about an hour later when Peter cuffed the new boy around the ears and took it back. It was just Peter. His affections came and went like glints on the iridescent scum of the water trough outside when the sun caught it.

A fair-weather friend, James's mother might have called him. But the memory made his heart hurt, so he tried to forget it. He never succeeded in forgetting, not like Peter could, but he could think of something else, and that worked as well.

Besides, Peter wasn't like that with James. At eight o'clock at night, after the work was done and the supper bowls licked clean, the boys would be shepherded upstairs to bed. In summer it was light yet, but for most of the year they lay down in darkness. The beds were hard and the covers thin. The children were so worn out that within minutes the sounds of shivering would merge into quiet breathing and snoring.

Except for Peter. His bed was next to James's, close enough on still nights for James to hear the strange tick-tock of his heart. When everybody else had settled, Peter's whisper would cross the space between them.

"James?" His voice sounded less cocky in the dark. "James, give us a story."

"What sort of a story?" James would ask, and Peter would say, "One about fairies"; or "Red Indians"; or "Mermaids"; and

just like that James was expected to begin. Fortunately, James knew a great many stories.

It was hard, sometimes. After a very long day, James was too sleepy to keep his eyes open, and yet if he closed them his voice would trail off in no time and he would wake with a start to Peter's cold hand on his shoulder. And Peter was very particular about the kinds of stories he wanted. They had to be adventure stories. They could be about adults—even Peter understood that most pirates were adults—but they couldn't contain what Peter called "grown-up rubbish," which meant no kissing, no crying, no parents, no sad endings. At his most unreasonable, he wouldn't allow endings at all. But James loved telling the stories. He loved the way the grim grey world would drop away and they could be somewhere bright and warm and colourful.

Peter would tell stories of his own at times, but that was different. Peter clearly didn't think of them as stories. Late at night he would talk about Kensington Gardens, which James knew vaguely to be on the other side of London, so distant from the workhouse that it might as well have been in another world. According to Peter, he had lived with the birds there when he was a baby. All children were once birds, he said—that was why nursery windows had bars on them, to stop them flying away. But his had been left open, and he had still remembered how to fly. Every night after lock-out time in the park, he would cross the Serpentine in a boat built by the thrushes, and play music for the fairies. James loved to hear about the fairies, but Peter was vague on details.

"I was only a week old," he explained airily.

"But you must have been there a long time," James protested. He knew it was all pretend, of course, but Peter took pretending very seriously. "You did so many things."

"I was a week old for a long time." Peter sat up with a bounce. "Anyway, there's nothing very interesting about fairies, once you get to know them. Let's have another story."

And nothing would do then but for James to find another story to tell them.

It didn't matter greatly if James ran out of stories of any particular kind, for he quickly learned that Peter, true to form, never seemed to remember that he'd been told a story before. For five nights in one month he was worried and thrilled by the fate of Cinderella, even though each time she put on the slipper in the exact same way and so claimed her prince. (They couldn't kiss, of course, so James had them merely hold hands and exchange gifts.) The great discovery, though, came on one winter's night when James was so weary that he couldn't remember any stories at all. Food had been short for the third day in a row, he was damp from the pitiless rain outside, and his frail little body ached all over. He desperately hoped that Peter, just this once, would be tired too and let him sleep. Peter, as always, was tireless.

"James," he whispered, as always. "Give us a story."

"Don't you want to sleep?" James tried. "It's well after dark."

"That's why," Peter said. "The darkness is too big. We need another story."

James sighed and closed his eyes for just a moment. There was a lump in his throat, and when he swallowed it, tears forced their way to his eyelashes. "What sort of a story?"

"One about pirates," Peter said.

James knew stories about pirates, just not at that moment. But Peter was waiting, and so, in desperation, he made one up.

"Once upon a time," he said, "on a far away island, there was a terrible pirate. He had been Blackbeard's bos'un, and the only man that Barbecue ever feared. He had a hook for a right hand, and when one of his pirate crew made him angry, he would rip them open with one swipe. It was this that earned him his last name, Hook. His first name was James."

In all the long nights, even those spent listening to Peter, James had never thought of being in the stories himself. He felt a thrill, and knew something powerful and magical had happened. Next to him, he heard Peter sit bolt upright.

"James," he said, and his voice was brimming with excitement. "What about me? Who's Peter?"

For a moment, James thought about making Peter a better, stronger pirate, but something in him rebelled. Just for once, he was the one in control, and he was the pirate. Although of course Peter would have to be something very grand.

"Peter lives on the island where James makes berth. He's the king of the island. He's called Peter Pan, because he has a pan flute, like the one I made you."

"That's not as good as being a pirate," Peter said, but uncertainly. James had never heard Peter sound uncertain before.

"It is." James was wide awake now. "Because he's not just a regular king. He's the spirit of the island. Everything on it is under his rule. He does nothing all day but have adventures with mermaids and Indians." Peter's silence was still unconvinced. On impulse, James added, "He can fly."

There was a sharp intake of breath, and for a moment James wondered if Peter was upset. In the days living with the birds in Kensington Gardens, Peter had said, he had been able to fly, and he missed it now. When he spoke again, though, his voice was filled with wonder.

"Go on," he demanded. "What do they do?"

From that night on, the very darkest and coldest nights were always given to stories about Captain James Hook and Peter Pan and their island. Sometimes they were friends, and sometimes enemies; it didn't seem to matter. It was a place they could go back to together, and nothing there ever changed.

They called it Neverland, for all the things that would never threaten them there. Never work. Never pain. Never fear. Never endings.

BUT THERE are always endings. This one came when Peter was thirteen, almost fourteen. James was twelve.

That night, as usual, James lay in bed and waited for the command to tell a story. He had one prepared. As he had bent over his work all day, picking oakum until his fingers bled, his mind had leaped to the ships the oakum would service, and from there to his own ship berthed at Neverland. All day, his

ship had sailed Mermaid Cove, and Peter had soared with it. He couldn't wait for it to become real as he whispered it into the dark.

But Peter gave no command. James listened for his voice, and heard instead the rise and fall of his breath. It was faster than usual.

James was almost asleep when he heard a rustle of blankets, and then a creak. He sat up in time to see Peter's shadow in the dark. It was between their two beds and moving away.

"Peter?" he whispered. "Peter, what are you doing?"

Peter's shadow paused. In another boy it would have been hesitation, but Peter never hesitated.

"Good-bye, James," he said, and bent down into a quick embrace. For a moment, he was pressed close enough that James could feel the now-familiar tick-tock of his heart. Then he was gone.

For a moment it really seemed as though he had disappeared, between one shadow and the next. Then James saw. Peter was at the window, one leg out and one leg in. Their room was on the top floor of the workhouse, directly beneath the rafters, but Peter seemed unaware of the dizzying drop below. He climbed out—and then, astonishingly, he climbed *up*.

James leapt out of bed to follow him. He never thought to do anything else.

It was cold on the roof; cold enough that James's fingers turned to ice and threatened to slip accordingly. The tile scraped his bare knees. Yet he gritted his teeth, and refused to look down. Peter stood on the ridge, light and agile as a cat.

"Where are you going?" James called.

Peter pointed. In the night sky, a light was burning. It must have been a star, but it was brighter than any star James had ever seen. And it was coming towards them.

"There! Second to the right, and straight on till morning!"

"I don't understand. What's there?"

The light from the star was on Peter's face. "Neverland."

James did look down then, against all his best intentions. The workhouse courtyard swam before his eyes, as if at the bottom of a very deep sea. He swallowed hard.

"There *is* no Neverland," he said. "I made it up."

"The fairies sent me here to grow up," Peter said. "But I don't want to grow up. I heard them talking, the superintendent and the matron. They want to move a bunch of us into the workhouse proper tomorrow, those of us who are fourteen or near enough. Once they do that I'll be a man. They'll set me to work in the factories, or they'll find me an apprenticeship, and if I can't keep up I won't eat. I'll fall between the cracks, and winter's coming. Do you know what happens to the ones who fall between the cracks when winter comes?"

It was the first time James had heard Peter so much as intimate he understood the possibility of death.

"Some of them live to grow old," he said. "Not all of them. But some."

"Not me," Peter said.

The light had reached them, and it was no star. It hovered about Peter, so brilliant and so glittering that Peter seemed to be glittering too, and then all at once he was. His skin

twinkled with gold dust. The light turned once around Peter's head, then headed out into the night.

Peter kicked his feet once, and launched himself after it. He flew.

James crouched, clinging to the roof, and watched Peter rise higher and higher into the sky, like a marionette being drawn up after a show was over. It was impossible. But he was seeing it. And his breath caught, because he was seeing Peter Pan.

"Peter!" he called. "Peter, come back!"

Peter didn't come back. He didn't even look back. He was flying away.

In that moment, James knew that if he couldn't fly away too, he didn't want to live. He didn't want to grow up day after painful day in the workhouse without Peter. He would rather die.

He put a hand on the chimney and raised himself upright. The wind tore at his clothes and brought with it a tingle of gold dust that made him cough. The courtyard below was a pool of shadows. The stars were bright and cold overhead.

"Take me with you!" he called. "Please!"

There was no answer.

Heart pounding, chest heaving, James turned his eyes upwards and jumped.

THEY FOUND him the next morning, barely breathing, crumpled and broken on the stones of the courtyard like a baby bird fallen from a nest. Peter was nowhere to be seen.

II
The Shadow

JAMES had not flown, but neither did he die. He lay on a hard bed for months in the workhouse infirmary, broken in a hundred places. Most of the time he dozed in a haze of pain, forcing himself to wake for water and food because he knew those feeding him would prefer he didn't.

"No use left in that one," he heard a young woman's voice say once. "That back won't mend. Best for everyone if he left this world."

Peter had left this world. James had seen him, flying on a river of gold dust. He would have given anything to follow. Instead, he climbed slowly and painfully back into the only world he had. He might not have made it, had it not been for two people.

The first was a doctor, a fact which under other circumstances wouldn't have been surprising. Doctors, after all, are often the reason bones set and bodies knit back together.

But there was little real medical treatment given at the workhouse. The sick were tended to by the Medical Officer, and even in some cases cared for, but for the most part they would either recover or not, and either way the infirmary would get the use of the bed back. And yet at the time James was there, Dr Matthew came once a week from the Great Ormond Street Children's Hospital to look in on the sick children.

At first, James knew only a gentle pair of hands and a soft voice: hands that curled around his sore wrist and turned him over to probe the agony in his spine, a voice that asked him to speak if something hurt and made reassuring noises when he moaned. Later, when his head began to clear and his eyes to regain their focus, he saw that the hands and voice belonged to a man who was small, almost like a child himself, with quick, deft movements and a well-groomed moustache. James was interested in very little still but his own loss and misery, and yet the doctor sparked a flicker of interest in him. He seemed, oddly, to care whether James lived or died.

Dr Matthew did care, and yet James sparked no unusual interest in him at first. Sick and injured children were so common in London that trying to save them was like trying to hold back a river using only bare hands. He was a very kind man, which was why he was there at his own time and expense, but he was also a very busy one, and it was doubtful he would have looked beyond James's injuries had he not discovered, quite by accident, that James could read.

"Thank you, Dr Matthew," James said weakly, when the doctor gave him a cup of something bitter to swallow that he said would make him feel better.

"You're very welcome, young man," the doctor replied, with a reassuring twinkle that masked his surprise. His voice had a pleasant cadence that James had no way of knowing was Scottish. "We've not really had the chance to speak before, have we? Did you ask someone my name?"

"It's on your stick." James managed to nod at the walking stick the doctor had propped beside the bed. There was a silver band with engraving just under the head, where the man's grip had worn away at the wood. "It says your name, and 'A gift from a grateful patient.'" He stumbled a little over the last two words, but that was mostly because his vision was blurry. It had only been two weeks since his fall. "I know the name Matthew, because my mother used to give me Matthew Arnold's poems."

"She taught you how to read?"

"She said that gentlemen should know how to read," James said. His eyes brimmed with unexpected tears then, and he had to close them quickly. He had not cried about his mother for a long time—he had told himself that he could survive her loss, now he had Peter. But now he had lost Peter, and yet he was still expected to go on just the same. He was fighting so hard to live, and he didn't know why. It was just a habit, that was all, and habits could be broken, like the bones in his back that everyone whispered would never be the same again. Like hearts.

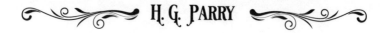

"There, there," the doctor's voice said softly, and a soft hand brushed James's hair from his forehead. "Don't cry, lad. While there's life there's hope."

He was called away then to another bed, and James fell into another heavy, miserable sleep without dreams. But neither forgot each other.

While there's life, there's hope, the doctor had said. The words were waiting for James when he woke, and they meant something. *While there's life.* Peter wasn't like his mother after all. He wasn't dead. He was only lost, and that meant he could be found again. James could find him, if he had to search the entire world, if it took until the end of his days. It was something to cling to, to pull himself out of despair, and he grabbed it and clung to it with all his heart. Life, and hope.

And James had said that he knew how to read. The next time Dr Matthew came, he came prepared. He was disgusted at himself for offering *while there's life there's hope* to a child lying orphaned and broken in an infirmary bed, and he was determined to give something more.

"I've brought you something to read," he said, before he even examined James's injuries. There were two books, beautifully bound, one a slim volume of Keats and the other a much heftier edition of *Robinson Crusoe*. James stared. The only books he had ever owned had been old penny dreadfuls his mother had bought him, and a battered Bible that had been sold for a handful of coins after her death. He had never in his life seen anything so solid or so reassuring or so beautiful as the pages encased in engraved leather.

"Thank you," he whispered. He wanted to take them up in his arms, but he was afraid to touch them with his dirty self.

"They're from my personal library," Dr Matthew said. "If you like them, and you take good care of them, I'll take them back and bring you new ones next week."

James nodded, unable to speak. He couldn't work out why such a thing had happened to him, in the very bleakest time of his life. It seemed a miracle. He never knew that the doctor had been haunted by the inadequacy of his response to James's grief, and Dr Matthew never knew that he needn't have been.

James did take care of the books, and what's more he loved them so thoroughly that Dr Matthew knew he really was reading them. Soon he was bringing him books every week, and not only stories but science, mathematics, memoirs. James liked the history books most of all. They were stories too in their way, and in their pages were bright, vivid characters who populated his imaginary world alongside Cinderella and Robin Hood. He had a particular fascination with Charles II, less for his personal qualities and more for his appearance. The doctor had looked over James's shoulder at the illustrations one day and remarked, half-teasingly, that the monarch looked rather like James himself.

"Do you think so?" James asked, peering at the drawing with interest. And it was true, he could see it now. At least, they had the same dark hair and eyebrows, pale skin, and narrow face. A deposed king, in exile and in hiding, ready to retake the throne. Once the idea had been given to him, he couldn't let it go.

It wasn't uncommon for workhouse children to be able to read. They were taught in schoolrooms, and the expectation was that by the time they left they should at least be able to sign their name. But James had a hunger for knowledge that was unusual, or at least usually soon trampled into London's grimy cobbles. He had ambition, too—or at least, for some half-remembered reason, he longed to be a gentleman. Sometimes the doctor would find a few stray minutes to sit by James's bed and regale him with stories of his own childhood at Eton, and James's face would glow.

"That's where you ought to be," the doctor said—sadly, James thought. In truth, there were days when Dr Matthew thought this work would break him. "There, or somewhere like it. But I'll see what can be done. At least those bones of yours are mending."

He *was* mending, in mind as well as body. What wasn't due to the books was due to the second person, and that person was Gwendolen Darling.

HE MET her for the first time when he was asleep. He was deep in a dream, the same dream he had over and over again, a dream of standing on the roof while Peter flew away, a dream in which he followed Peter through the trees and oceans and adventures of Neverland knowing he would never reach it himself. Only this time, right when Peter was rounding the

crest of the second star to the right, he felt a sharp dig in his ribs. He opened his eyes, startled, to find a girl looking down at him.

"You were crying," she said matter-of-factly. She, unlike Peter, had no curiosity about why. It was the workhouse. Everyone cried.

He rubbed his eyes, still half-asleep, and found them damp with tears. It was dark, and all he could see of the girl was glimpses lit by a single candle.

"Sorry," he said, and she shrugged and moved away. He went back to sleep, weary and feverish, and didn't dream again.

He thought of her the following day, and as the evening lengthened into night he watched to see if she would come back. She did. As the matron left for the night, she came to take her shift, dressed in workhouse grey with her dark hair pinned up. When she looked at him, his chest gave a jolt, as if something that had stopped when Peter left had started again.

She must have been fourteen, or she would have been in the children's quarters and not helping in the infirmary. But she looked younger, as half-starved workhouse children often did. She was a thin, pale creature, sharp-edged and quick-eyed, wary and clever and fragile as a wild animal. She looked, in short, very much like James, and even though she was a girl he felt he *knew* her. Though he might have imagined it, he thought she knew him too.

"What's your name?" he asked her, when she passed by his bed.

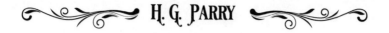

She stopped. "Gwendolen Jane Darling," she said. "What's yours?"

"James," he said.

"That it? Just James?"

"That's it," he said firmly. He had never known his father's surname, and now that his mother was dead he didn't want the name of the family that had left her to die on the streets. The workhouse had given him a surname when he came in, but he didn't want that either.

"Fair enough," she said. "Keep it down, James, all right? There's folk trying to sleep."

But the infirmary was only sparsely inhabited at that time, and she didn't really mind. After an hour or so, when it was clear that he wasn't going to sleep himself, he felt the bed creak and give as she sat at its foot. He sat, painfully, and saw her pick up the top-most of Dr Matthew's books from the pile. (As it happened, it was the first volume of *Ivanhoe*.)

"How's this, then?" she asked. "Any good?"

She was only just fourteen, he learned that night, and an orphan as he was. Her father had been an apothecary, which is why they had her watch the women and children's wards at night, but she didn't like it. She could never sleep lightly, so she stayed awake all night and was exhausted all her days. She didn't like the pain or the sickness or the death. It was better than starving, she said, but so were most things.

What she liked, it turned out, were stories, just as Peter had, although in every other respect she was as little like Peter as it was possible to be. She could read too, but since she had

to work all day while James was in bed it was easier if he read them and told them back to her. And so he found himself once again whispering words into the dark, feeling them take on their own life and become something more real than the world around him. In the light of them, the darkness was once again not quite so big.

He didn't tell her about Neverland. It was for Peter's ears alone—besides, once he got to know her better, he realised she wouldn't have been interested. She wasn't interested in the stories of Eton that Dr Matthew gave him either, though she allowed him to relate them to her occasionally once she saw how badly he wanted to repeat them aloud. She liked history better, and so he told her about James II and Queen Elizabeth, then about Cleopatra and the Romans and the discovery of America. What she really liked, though, was to hear about other countries, other oceans, the journey that he planned to make by ship one day when he left the workhouse. He did his best to give her what she needed: the feel of the waves cresting under the ships, the ever-changing skies, the hot, boisterous ports of Spain and Trinidad and the South Pacific. She liked the islands best, and he tried to summon them to the cold, damp building in the middle of a London winter.

"I never understand why you like hearing about a school full of rich boys when you have all that to look forward to," she said to him one night. There was a storm washing the dirty streets outside, and rain drummed against the roof and lashed the windows.

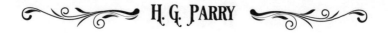

"I should have been one of those rich boys," he said. It was a secret part of his heart that he'd never even told to Peter. "My mother used to tell me my father was a gentleman."

"Was? Is he dead?"

He shrugged in the dark. "She told me he died when I was a baby and they were newly married. But I'm not sure they were ever married in the first place. She used to tell me stories about being in service to a wealthy family. The stories stop just before I was born, and she died on the streets." The ones who fall through cracks, Peter had said. There were so many cracks in the world.

"The bastard." Gwendolen hugged her knees, and for a moment was uncharacteristically quiet. "You're better off without him, James. Believe me. You'll be free of all it on the sea."

"I don't think there's a lot of freedom on the sea," he said. "It just makes for some good stories."

"You're good at stories." It was a rare compliment from her. "You bring them to life, somehow."

"My friend Peter used to love stories," he said.

"The boy who ran away the night you jumped from the roof? What happened to him? People are saying he jumped too, but he died."

"He didn't die," James said, a little too sharply. "He's lost. I'll find him one day. Across the world, in the depths of the ocean, beyond the bounds of the sky if I have to. I'll find him."

Gwendolen, wisely, said nothing to this. James was a different sort of boy to those she'd talked to before, kind and sensitive and gentle, but she'd already learned that at times a

hard light would kindle in his eyes, and at those times it was best to leave him alone until it died.

James's feeling that Gwendolen and he were alike was not entirely founded. They had certain base elements in common, it was true, but at her core she was laughter and insults and fiery temper, and he was something that burned altogether colder and stranger. His feeling that she knew him on sight was not entirely founded either. She didn't know him—in some ways she never would. But she liked him from the first.

BECAUSE JAMES did not die, he grew up. By the end of his thirteenth year he was walking again, with barely a limp to show for his adventure.

Things were easier for him than they had been. He found himself on lighter work duties than before, not because of his injuries, but because of his education. He was a useful person to have in a schoolroom, or even helping with records and correspondence. Dr Matthew told the workhouse board that he might well be able to find a position for James as a clerk when he was a little older, and to take good care of him.

And this might, in fact, have been his future, had it not been for Peter. Dr Matthew had come just a little too late. Before he could give James an object to work towards, James's brain had already fixed on another: to find Peter at all costs. By day he worked, and studied when the long, harsh hours of labour would allow it. By nights, he searched his dreams of Neverland

for his lost friend. Dreams were no good, though, he knew that. The star would not come for him, as it had for Peter. He needed to leave the workhouse, leave London, and find his own way to Neverland. It was the rope he had seized to keep him tethered to the world, and now he couldn't let it go. At times he wished he could forget as easily as Peter did. But it was no use. His body remembered, and his back always ached more on cold nights when the stars were high.

James was set to be moved from the children's quarters at fourteen. He didn't wait that long. The day before, he left the workhouse in the cool light of the morning and made his way through the grimy streets to the banks of the Thames.

He was barely out of the great iron gates when he heard a cry from behind him.

"James!"

He turned, and saw at first a tall, skinny boy running towards him. He wore a ragged grey flannel shirt and dark trousers held up with braces; his face was shadowed by a rough tweed cap under which dark hair could be seen. Then the boy drew close, panting, and he saw that it was Gwendolen Darling.

James hadn't seen her in a year, since he had been released from the infirmary. Men and women and children were kept strictly separate: he had not so much as glimpsed her in the dining hall. His chest gave the same shudder of recognition it had given the first time he had ever noticed her, and this time something in it opened and would never close again.

Gwendolen was oblivious to all of this as she caught him up. "I want to come with you," she said. "I've been thinking

it through for months. Then I heard you were leaving, and I thought I'd missed my chance. With my hair cut we could easily pass for brothers."

"Why?" His heart, poor human thing that it was, was racing. "Why would you want to come with me?"

"Because I want to go to sea." Her face a few inches from his was intent, her eyes like fixed stars. "I want to get away from this place, now. I want to go to those places you told me about."

James could almost have laughed. It seemed to him so peculiar that every person he loved ended up loving his stories more—that all of them, in the end, wanted to run away to the places he gave them and not to stay by his side. And yet Gwendolen, at least, wanted him to go with her.

"They won't take a girl," Gwendolen was saying. "But they'll take two boys—and if you do the talking, they won't look so closely at me. And in return, I can help you. You're a clever lad, James, but you don't know the world the way I do. There are fortunes to be made at sea, and we can make one. I know we can."

She was deathly serious, defiant even. For a moment, he felt almost afraid of her.

James didn't want to make his fortune. He wanted to go to sea for one reason only: he wanted to find Peter again, if he had to travel beyond the ends of the earth. But he didn't want to be alone. He had been alone on the night his mother died, on the night Peter had flown away, on many nights since he had been released from the infirmary. It was sharp

and cold and terrible, like being without a limb. He wanted Gwendolen's warmth and her cleverness and her matter-of-fact laugh. He was even starting to suspect he might want her in other ways, ways Peter would have called grown-up rubbish, ways that he wasn't quite ready to think about yet but wanted to later, very much.

Besides, he wasn't a fool. He was sharp enough to see the sense in what she was proposing—or, more accurately, the possibilities. Gwendolen did know things that he didn't, the kind that couldn't be learned in books. She had lived in the outside world for a lot longer than he had, and seen a great deal more of it at her father's side. She understood it in ways he did not, and probably never would. That could only help in his quest as well as in hers. He might, if he played his cards right, even be a captain one day.

"All right," he said. "We'll go together."

SHIPS WERE clustered in the great pool of the harbour—not the glorious pirate ships of his dreams, but freight ships, steamboats, clippers, brigs and schooners of the East India Company being loaded with cargo and bound for foreign shores. It was a week before they found one looking for two cabin boys.

"What's your name, lad?" the bo'sun asked him.

"James," he said, and watched the man write it down. He could write his own name, but didn't mention it. Perhaps they wouldn't want a cabin boy who could write. "This is my brother George."

The bo'sun's eyes flickered casually to Gwendolen's face, and James held his breath. If there was ever a moment when this would not work, it would be now.

He needn't have worried. The man's eyes glanced off Gwendolen's face like a stone skimming water. "Last name?"

James didn't know his surname. Gwendolen didn't want hers to help them be found. And so they joined the crew of the *Kirriemuir* under the name of Hook.

III

COME AWAY, COME AWAY

FIRST Mate James Hook had almost forgotten the star when he saw it again.

He was a very long way away from the workhouse rooftop in London—in frigid Arctic waters, under a clear cold night sky, on the deck of the whaling ship *White Bird*. The deck was almost deserted, most of the crew asleep. Bill Jukes was at the helm, tattooed arms strong at the wheel; Skylights the cabin boy was assisting. Captain Patrick Smithers had come up only an hour ago for a final check before leaving James on watch. He was a stout, formidable man, weathered by storms and salt winds, but James had been two years at sea with him and knew how to spot the twinkle in his eye.

"Bloody freezing tonight, Hook," Smithers had said. As always, his Connacht lilt made the complaint sound cheerful. "All in order up here?"

"Yes, Captain," James agreed, on both counts. The seas were quiet, and in the darkness they could have been a great frozen pond with the white caps of the waves drifts of snow.

Smithers blew on his hands, stamped the ice from his boots, and stifled a yawn. "Well, I'll leave you to it, then. Good night, Hook."

"Goodnight, Captain."

"I'll be down below if you need me."

"Yes, Captain."

"Don't you dare need me."

"No, Captain."

Smithers chuckled, and James heard his steady pace move to the hatch. In his wake, the world above was still as if frozen. The stars were dazzling against the blue-black sky, and the waves were glass.

It had been a long time since the workhouse rooftop too—almost twenty years, and James had spent most of them trying to become a different person. It had been easier than he could have imagined, at least on the outside. Money could be earned, and it could buy better clothes. His body could grow, and did, and with it his face had lost its starved, haunted quality and his voice had deepened and lost its street twang. His past could be altered to match, just by telling a story. He was James Hook now, not a workhouse orphan but the younger son of a gentleman, educated at Eton but fallen on hard times. The crew of the *White Bird* were fond of him, with his thoughtful nature and odd flashes of temper. It was true his ideas were a little old-fashioned (the way he grew his black

hair long and curled, for instance, in a style more befitting a dandy of the last century than a working man in the modern world), and they had their suspicions as to whether a gentleman born and bred at Eton could really have wound up first mate of a common whaling ship as easily as he claimed. But they accepted it, because he could tell so many stories about it, and they liked to hear them.

The difficult parts were inside. Fortunately, nobody cared about those, except perhaps Gwendolen, and in his darkest moments he even wondered about her.

He was a good seaman. It was no innate skill—in fact, the first time he'd stepped on a boat he discovered he was horribly seasick and hated being wet. He was clever and focused: he would have been good at whatever he'd set his mind to, and so he was good at this. But he wouldn't have advanced the way he had if it had not been for Gwendolen. Gwendolen had become a different person in ways he couldn't imagine. After all these years, to everyone but him she was still George Hook, jaunty and reckless and strong for his size. She liked being George, she said. George, after all, could pull in a man's wage—there were women on many ships, but in the capacity of wives and not workers. George knew everything that James didn't: which ships were making berth, where they were headed, which captains would make their crew a fortune and which would get them all killed. It was George who had secured them their positions as high-ranking officers on board the *White Bird*, and Gwendolen had promised James that this would be it.

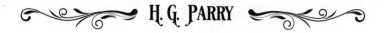

"Trust me," she said, their last time on shore. "Eight more months at sea, and then we'll have enough to live off for years. There's a fortune to be made in whaling with a captain who knows what he's doing—and Smithers is one of the best there is."

He did trust her, now as always. She had proven to be right in the past, and would again.

They had only one ongoing argument, which was that she was a thief. Not in a major way, and never on their ships—she stole trinkets from public houses when there were enough guests that they would never be blamed, picked the pockets of an occasional drunken officer at busy ports. It unsettled him. He wasn't afraid she would be caught: she was too clever and too charming for that. He just didn't feel that it was good form.

"Good form?" she laughed, incredulous, when he tried to explain. "James, good form is some rubbish that Dr Matthew told you as a bedtime story when you were a child. It's just as made-up as class or blood or manners or anything else they teach at Eton. We're already stealing by pretending to be someone we're not."

"But we're *not* pretending." He tried to find the right words. "We've become those people now. We are James and George Hook, younger sons of an Eton-educated gentleman who have fallen on hard times. James and George Hook wouldn't steal."

She gave him a very peculiar look. "You *are* a strange one sometimes. Well, if James Hook ever wants to get out of those hard times into which he's fallen, then he's going to have to let George steal. We need the money."

He didn't argue with that, although they both knew it wasn't true. Gwendolen didn't really steal because they needed the money. She stole because she needed the feeling of security it gave her, the knowledge that if she was left with nothing again she could still take what she needed to survive. She stole to feel safe. James envied her that. He had never in his life found anything to make him feel safe.

James walked up and down the deck in the dark night, trying to keep his limbs from stiffening, wincing at the familiar ache in his back. He thought, half wistful and half resentful, of Gwendolen curled up warm in her own bunk. She was second mate, largely because she was supposed to be younger than him, yet somehow she knew how to stay off the bitter night watches. His thoughts were very far away when a flicker of light against his eyes brought him back.

Something in the sky. Something quicksilver and bright, something that he had seen before, a very long time ago. Something from when he was a boy.

A boy standing on a rooftop, watching Peter fly away.

"Look at that, sir," Bill Jukes said, but he didn't need to. James was already staring straight up, where a light brighter than any star was coming towards them.

James and Gwendolen had travelled the world over the last twenty years. They had been on ships trading tea and wine and coal, grain and timber and rice; they had chased whales across the coldest and wildest oceans. They had seen the skies of China and of New York, of Burma and San Francisco and the Pacific Northwest. Thousands of nights of stars, and none of them had ever contained the one James sought. The thought had started to intrude, burrowing through his defences like a pebble through a shoe, that perhaps none of them ever would. On black nights, when his defences were particularly thin, he wondered if he had imagined the whole thing. He had fallen from a roof on that night, after all. Against his will, he had started to doubt.

But now it was here. The star had found him.

It was like waking from a sleep, or a daydream. He had never wanted to be a merchant sailor, or the first mate of a whaling ship. He had never even wanted to make his fortune. He had wanted to be a pirate.

"Turn the ship around," he said.

Bill Jukes was still looking at the star in awe mingled with superstitious fear. It took him a moment to turn and look at him. "Sir? On what heading?"

James didn't return the look. His eyes were fixed ahead. "Follow that star."

Second to the right and straight on till morning.

Neverland.

THE CREW felt the ship begin to change course. James didn't bother to look—he couldn't take his eyes from the star—but he heard the sound of voices below, footsteps coming up on deck. The only reason for such a sudden, drastic alteration would be a whale sighted, and no such cry of "thar she blows!" had gone up from the masts.

"What the bloody hell is going on?" It was Captain Smithers, pulling a salt-stained coat over a thick jumper, still blinking sleep from his eyes. "Hook?"

"I've changed our course, Captain."

"Why? To what heading?"

"That star. Look at it." Dimly, he was aware of more men on deck behind the captain. One of them was George, Gwendolen, her face pale and white and wide-eyed in the light of the lanterns. In that moment, she was dim to his eyes as well. "I've seen it before, when I was very young. A friend of mine—it took him. It took him beyond the edge of the world. We need to follow it."

"James," Gwendolen said, very carefully. She alone knew what he was talking of, and dread crept into her heart. "You need to—"

Smithers silenced her with a warning look. "Are you trying to tell me you've changed course to chase after a bloody star?"

Even in his heightened state, James had just enough reason not to say what he suspected the star really was. "Yes, Captain."

"We're not the three wise men, Hook! This is a whaling ship. We chase after baleen and oil and blubber, not lights in the sky."

"You don't understand—it isn't the light we need. It will take us to an island. An island with everything we could ever want."

He could hear his voice, normally so controlled, sounding broken, frantic, upset. Smithers must have heard it too. His own voice softened, as if talking to a child. "There are no islands in these parts, James. Not for miles. I think you and I need to go below decks for a chat. Jukes, turn us back around."

Before either of them could blink, the pistol was in James's hand, primed and ready to fire. Afterwards, that fact was more surprising to James than it was to Smithers. He had never in his life done anything of the kind before. At the time, he felt nothing about it. All he felt was the distance, painful and tugging and increasing, between himself and the star; all he saw when he looked at his captain was an obstacle between them.

"Jukes," he said quietly, "belay that order. Captain, there's no time to talk. We need to follow that star now, or we'll lose it again. Trust me."

"Trust you, is it? And what if I don't trust you one bit?"

"We're going after that star, Captain. Or so help me I will shoot you myself, right here."

Smithers looked in his eyes, and saw in them the hard glitter that Gwendolen had recognised so long ago. She knew it as a sign to back down; Smithers should have known it too. But for some reason, he didn't. Perhaps he had seen it too often, on too many other English gentlemen in his life. Instead, he raised his head, and his kind eyes held a glint of their own.

"We're not, lad," he said. "If you back down right now, I will set you off at the next port and there will be no more word about this. If not, you'll be turned over to the authorities when we get home. That's the best I can do for you. I like

you, and I always have. But this is my ship, and by God I'll not stand by and let you take it on some damn-fool path off the edge of the world."

James shot him.

It was no more conscious than the decision to bring out the pistol in the first place. His finger spasmed on its own accord. Somewhere deep in his chest, alarm spiked; deep in his ears, a voice was screaming *no, no, stop it*. But the far greater part of him felt nothing. He needed to follow the star—he *needed* to. There was so little time. He watched Smithers choke, crumple, fall heavily to the ground drawing his last breaths through blood, and saw only an obstacle cleared from his way.

The men on deck watched in horror. It wasn't Smithers's death that horrified them, though they liked and respected him. They had seen many deaths at sea, many brutal punishments, even a few murders. It was the first mate. For just an instant, as he had fired the pistol, the light in his eyes had gleamed red. He had seemed another person, one they did not recognise at all.

"This is my ship," that person said to them. "I'm the captain now. And we will maintain the same heading. Any other objections?"

There were none. There were twenty of them and one of him, but nobody else dared move, not even Gwendolen.

"Take the body to the brig," Captain Hook said. He didn't pause to watch his order carried out, although he knew that it was. He took the helm himself. The ship turned towards the path of the star.

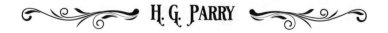

THE DAWN came, but the star refused to dim. It burned in the pale blue sky, hotter than the sun. James's ship pursued it. A storm blew up, blackening the sky like a bruise then slashing it with rain. The star burned still, through hail and cloud, and still the *White Bird* pursued it.

Straight on till morning, Peter had said. It hadn't meant anything. Peter had always just said whatever came into his head.

Gwendolen was waiting for James when he came down to his cabin to change. He had avoided coming below as long as possible, knowing she wouldn't argue with him on deck in front of everyone at the risk of exposing her own secret, knowing he would have to face her in the end.

"James, what the *hell* are you doing?"

"You know what I'm doing," he said briskly. He rifled through his sea-chest, avoiding her eyes. The irony was, there was little point in changing. Anything he changed into would be soaked in moments. He might as well have stayed on deck. He just hated to wear the same clothes for more than a day. It was bad form for a gentleman, and now he was a captain.

"Have you gone mad?" She had been sitting in his bunk, knees drawn up to her chest; now he heard the thud of her booted feet as she stood. "You can't really think you're going to find Peter, after all these years? By chasing a *star*?"

"It isn't really a star. And yes. I'll find him. This is what I've been looking for my whole life. It was why I went away to sea. You always knew that."

"You were a *child* then. I thought you'd grown up and seen sense!"

"Grown up?" He laughed, and it hurt. "I never had the chance to be anything but grown up. Nor did you. We were born into poverty and drudgery and filth, and that's exactly what being grown up is. Peter was right not to want it, all those years ago. I don't want it either."

"And what about what the rest of this ship wants? Does that matter at all?"

He heard her stop, draw breath. It was the way she always stopped to collect herself, and his chest ached at the familiarity of it.

"The ship can't take much more of this storm," she said, in a calmer tone. "We have to go back."

"Because of a storm?" James shook his head, and his wet curls fell in his face. "I jumped off a roof to follow Peter. I thought I was jumping to my death. A storm is nothing."

"You only hurt yourself on that roof, not the crew. Not me. I've never known you to put lives at risk like this. You're usually the first to hold back the whaleboats when things look dangerous. The men like you for it, because they trust you not to get them killed."

It was true. Whaling was a dangerous business—so was all sailing—and he had never had a death on his watch. But this was different. This wasn't about profit or making quota or shipping times. This was everything. "They *will* be safe, I promise. Once we get to Neverland, you'll understand. It isn't just about me. This is best for everyone."

"Everyone? Smithers is *dead*, James! James—look at me!" Her hand was on his shoulder, wrenching him to face her. "He's dead. You *killed* him."

"I didn't mean that to happen!" His numbness wore off then, just a little, and grief and guilt stabbed him for the first time. "I'm truly sorry it did. But I can't bring him back now. I've taken command. I need to hold it. I need everyone to be with me, or we'll never get there." He looked her in the eye for the first time. "Are *you* with me?"

She laughed, scornful, but with an edge of defiance that twisted his stomach. It was too obviously the defiance that came in the face of fear. "What would you do if I said no? Would you kill me too? You can hardly let me go on my way, miles from shore."

"No. But I hoped you would say yes."

"You said yes to me twenty years ago, James Hook!" She made the name a hiss. "I promised you we could make our fortunes."

"Is that what we've been doing?" Anger bit into his own voice. "Making our fortunes? Because it seems to me we're struggling to survive on a floating slaughterhouse."

"You seemed happy enough with our life before last night."

"I hate every minute of it!" On another day, he would have known it wasn't true, not quite. He hated a good many things, but not all of it. Not the Arctic waters cold and black under an endless sky. Not the salt wind in their sails and on their faces on a clear day. Not the men, Captain Smithers first among them, rowdy and cheerful and ready to celebrate any

small victory. Not Gwendolen. Never her. But he was in no mood to think of such things. "I hate the cold and the wet and the filth. I hate rowing out there watching a whale die for days at a time. I hate the blood and the oil and the butchery. I hate knowing there isn't another way."

"So you're throwing it all away on a childhood fantasy."

"It isn't a fantasy. It was once, I admit, but then it became something more. I saw that star take Peter off that roof, Gwendolen. I saw him fly, just as I said he could in the stories. He said he was going to Neverland. I know it sounds impossible, but I know it isn't. I saw it."

"You fell off a roof that night. You're fortunate to remember anything. You can't trust the memories you have."

"It isn't just that night." He hesitated, knowing how it would sound, then pressed ahead. "Peter always used to say that he lived in Kensington Gardens when he was a week old. He said he lived with birds and…and with fairies." There it was. He didn't look at her as he said it. "I never believed him, of course. I knew there were no fairies, and if there were, how could Peter remember what happened to him at one week old? It made no sense. They were just stories too, like Neverland. And then, last year, I went to Kensington Gardens. It was the first time we had been back in London since the workhouse, do you remember? I had never been to Kensington at all. It was evening, almost lock-out time. I went through the gates. And it was exactly as Peter had described it."

Her brow arched. "You saw fairies in Kensington Gardens?"

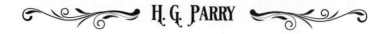

"No, of course not. But I saw the Round Pond and the Broad Walk, the Hump and the Baby Walk and Picnic Street. I saw everything Peter described. He had been a workhouse child his entire life. How could he have been to Kensington Gardens?"

"Many ways! He might have been taken there when he was being fostered. He might have run away from the workhouse and come back. He might have heard someone describe it, and took the story for his own."

"Or," James said, "he might have been raised there by the birds and fairies. And those same fairies might have come back for him, and taken him to Neverland."

He expected her to scoff then, or argue, or tell him he was mad, or push him away and storm out of the cabin. Instead, Gwendolen was silent, searching his face as if trying to see something beyond the new glimmer in his eyes.

"Answer me this," she said at last. "I want to understand. Assuming all this is true—assuming there are fairies, and a magic island, and your childhood best friend really did fly away the night you fell from a roof and it wasn't all a dream—why does it matter? Why does it mean so much to you that you'd give up everything else?"

The question stopped him short, as Peter's first question had stopped him short a long time ago, because the answer seemed so obvious. And yet this time, as he turned it over in his head, he realised that it wasn't. Because he loved the Neverland he had built, and needed it to be real again. Because he loved Peter, despite his many flaws and cruelties, and he needed him to be alive. Because James had latched on

to finding them both as a reason to live when he had no other, and he was afraid of what would happen to him if he let them go. All those were true, but they weren't the whole truth.

"Because," he answered at last, "that star took Peter away, all those years ago. It didn't take me too. It left me behind, and I grew up a workhouse orphan."

This, of all things, Gwendolen understood. "But that was then. You grew up a long time ago. You don't need to be rescued anymore."

"But I should have been. Do you know how that feels? I spent two more years in that place, two years of cold and hunger and sickness and hard work. My whole life since has been toil and filth. And all that time, I should have been in Neverland."

"You should have been at Eton too, according to you. That's why you always liked to hear about it so much, isn't it? That's why you insist on telling everyone that you grew up there instead." She shook her head. "You've got to stop this. You can't spend your whole life chasing after a past that was never yours. So what if you spent all those years in the workhouse? You escaped it in the end. We have the whole ocean now. We're free."

"I'm not free. I still live in that place. However far I go and whoever I try to be, I carry it inside me, every day. If you turned me inside out, I'd be smoke stacks and grey walls and picking oakum in a cold yard. The only time I've ever been free was when Peter would ask me for a story in the dark, and I would take us both to Neverland."

"And if you turned me inside out I'd be the same. Who cares? You move on as best you can, you learn what you can from it, but nobody escapes their past entirely."

"Peter does. He has no past. He never has. He has no sorrow, no memory, no pain."

"He sounds awful," Gwendolen said, accurately.

James sighed. He was worn to the bone, and his back ached. His soul ached too. Sometimes he thought that had been broken as well that night, along the same join.

(It hadn't. That would come later.)

Perhaps Gwendolen saw what she was looking for, because she sighed as well. "I'm with you," she said. "I'm with you because we've been together a long time now, and you trusted me when most wouldn't have. But I think you've gone insane."

James kissed her forehead, so grateful for her consent he barely heard the words of it. "You'll see. You'll see, if you only stay with me."

"I'll stay," she said. She didn't return his kiss, but she didn't move away from it either. "For now."

"And I'd never kill you," he added, as an afterthought. "You know that, don't you?"

She said nothing.

THEY CAUGHT the star in the dark before dawn on the third day. James had perched for hours on the prow of the ship, his hands poised. When it came near enough to snatch it, his

fingers inside his gloves were almost too cold to grasp, and the star almost too hot. But he held on.

It was a fairy, of course.

The fairy was perhaps three inches tall, and made of light. It buzzed in the cage of James's hands like an angry firefly.

"Take me to Neverland," James said.

The fairy couldn't talk, only chime a single note. In the end, they fastened it in a cage to the front of the ship, and followed the pointing of its tiny finger. James hoped Gwendolen would have more faith now she had seen it, but the sight of it did nothing to reassure her. It wasn't that she didn't believe it existed—she had to. She just didn't trust it.

"It could be leading you anywhere," she said. "I'm not even convinced it can understand you."

"It knows what I want," he said. "It's taking me where I want to go."

"We're running out of supplies. The crew are terrified. They think we're going to die."

"They'll feel differently when they get there," he said. "There's no fear there, and no death."

Gwendolen looked at him as if for the first time. Her arguments died from her eyes. "My God," she said quietly. "You really are insane."

(He wasn't, quite. That would come later too.)

STRAIGHT ON till morning. It was many nights, and many mornings. The food almost ran out, as Gwendolen predicted, and several of the men tried to refuse to go any further. But they had gone off the edge of the map, and it was too late to go back. They stayed on course. They followed the star off the edge of the world.

And perhaps Peter's instructions had meant something after all, because it was by the pale light of sunrise that they first saw the island.

IV
THE ISLAND COME TRUE

I T was a small island, by the standards of the British Navy. It would have taken their ship less than an hour to circumnavigate it. And yet the island defied any such classification. It was immense. Mountains plunged through the middle, piercing the sky; enormous waterfalls spilled down the rocks and crags to the sea. It was covered in trees, dark and green and no kind known to modern science. The edges were crinkled with pale sandy beaches, honeycombed with caves. It was a child's drawing of an island, a geography that made no sense until you realised that it was crammed with every possible setting for adventure. The men had never seen anything like it.

James hadn't slept in as long he could remember—he hadn't dared to lose sight of the fairy, and he hadn't dared to take his eyes off the mutinous crew. His eyes ached, and his bones were hollow with fatigue. And yet at the sight of the

cloud-covered mountains and white shores, something fierce and sweet thrilled in his chest.

"Take us to port," he told Jukes. "There's a lagoon around that cliff where we can make berth."

"How do you know that?" Jukes asked.

James didn't answer.

The crew's excitement died as they rounded the corner, and James's thrill faltered with it. It was too quiet. The lagoon waters were still; there was no wind, and no sound of birds. Even the fairy in the jar had stopped buzzing and fluttering.

Gwendolen had come to stand beside him on the deck. "Is this Neverland?" she asked.

She spoke in little more than a whisper, and he replied in the same tone. "Yes. It has to be. This is the mermaids' lagoon; the natives make their camp on that mountain. But—"

In the still, dead morning, a cry rang out over the island. It was a high, wild cry, like the crow of a cock, but the voice that shaped it was no bird's. It raised the hairs on James's neck, and several of the men muttered and shuffled their feet.

Gwendolen's voice for the first time held a tremble of fear. "What *was* that?"

"It's him." James's certainty had returned. "It's Peter."

"It didn't sound human."

"No." He turned back to Jukes, who was staring wide-eyed, pale beneath his burnished tan. "Prepare to drop anchor. We're here."

Heartless

THE BEACH was a gentle curve, the sand fine and powdery and soft until it gave way to rocks and lush green trees. Those trees were laden with fruit, and the sound of a stream nearby was like the burble of a song. After their long weeks of cold and fear and privation, it was like coming to paradise. The men forgot their worries about their strange new captain and the bloodstained way he had taken command. They ran through the warm water to the shore, laughing and whooping with joy.

They were so happy that they ran right into the arms of the waiting tribe of warriors.

THEY WEREN'T the Red Indians from James's stories. By that name, he had meant the caricatures he had met in penny dreadfuls, the only sort he had known as a child. In the intervening years, he had learned at least a little better, enough to know that the people those books described did not exist. There had been three Algonquins on the last whaling ship they had worked on—he had come to know them over six long months, and even to speak a few phrases of their language. And these people were not from Canada or America at all—they had the strong, broad features of some of the warriors he'd met and traded with in the Pacific Islands. Their grass skirts and intricate feather cloaks, too, reminded him of those people, though the green and yellow feathers were a kind he'd never seen before.

Their camp, too, was no camp at all but a village: storehouses, large huts woven of flax, a meeting house with a carved

front. It was perched halfway up the mountain, its gates and fortifications hidden from the beach. Their lookouts would have seen the *White Bird* coming from a great distance, James realised as he and his crew were bundled up the steep path. The war party, ten men carrying spears and knives made of bone, would have been sent to wait for them. They had never stood a chance.

They made no attempt to speak to James and the others, but nor were they violent. They nudged them through the rocks and scrub, grabbing them and hauling them back into line if they tried to run but not otherwise. Once inside the village, they were pushed roughly to their knees in the dirt. A crowd had gathered to watch them, eyes wide and curious. James, struggling for breath after the climb, saw a young girl of no more than four or five peeking from her mother's side, and tried to find her a smile. Plainly it was more scary than pleasant, because she hid her face, aghast.

"We mean you no harm," James said to the nearest man. "Please, can we just—?"

"Be quiet," the man said, not unkindly, and James was so surprised to hear his own language that he obeyed at once. Plainly, they were waiting for something.

They didn't have long to wait. The crowds were already parting, as if for a captain or dignitary. The woman who emerged could have been either or both. She was tall and well built, her brown face lined with wrinkles, her black hair shot through with grey, her shoulders strong beneath her cloak of white feathers. Her eyes were kind, James thought with perhaps more hope than accuracy, but her expression gave nothing away.

"Do you understand me?" the woman said. Her English was perfect, without a trace of accent.

Less startled this time, James nodded.

"I thought so," she said. "The lost boys don't speak our language either, nor we theirs, and yet we seem to understand one another. The spirits' doing, I assume. Are you the leader of these men?"

The memory of Smithers flashed into his head, but he nodded once more. "My name is James Hook." He hesitated, trying to think of something that wouldn't sound foolish. "We mean you no harm," he said, foolishly.

She raised her eyebrows. "I hope not, for your sake. You're not very good at it." She relented, with the pity of someone realising that their companion will never understand a joke. "We mean you no harm either, if that's true. But this is a dangerous island, and we couldn't have you on the beach for our safety and yours. My name is Tiare. I'm the leader of this village. I suppose the two of us should talk."

Gwendolen, beside him, nudged him sharply. He wished she wouldn't—he would have remembered her without the bruises. "May I bring my—my first mate?"

"You may," she allowed. "But the rest of your men will remain here, under guard. I'll bring them food and water, seeing as you look half-starved, but that's it. You're a bit larger than the boys the spirits usually bring. I don't want you making trouble."

"We won't," James said. "Thank you."

"Your kind always say you won't," the chief said, not without amusement, "when we have our spears on you."

THE MEETING house was dark and cool—mercifully so, after the blazing heat outside. Thirsty as he was, and light on sleep, James had been starting to feel dizzy. It was a relief, even under the circumstances, to take off his boots, sit down on woven mats, and accept a bowl of water. Gwendolen, beside him, did the same.

The chief sat in front of them. "You both look very tired," she said, matter-of-factly. "And very dirty. I assume you came from a long way away."

"We came from the Arctic," James said. He was testing her, but he saw not a flicker of recognition in her face. "And before that we set sail from Portsmouth, in England."

"And how did you come to be here?"

Smithers falling, choking. The star burning in his fingers. "We followed a star. A star that moved."

"A spirit, you mean. That was a reckless thing to do, if you had any choice in the matter." She looked at him closely, her eyes dark in her weathered face. "And it led you here, to our shores."

"Yes. To Neverland."

"If that's what you call it. Our own word for it is slightly different."

"Which is?"

"Home," she said flatly, and he couldn't decide whether she was making a point or whether whatever magic was translating their languages had done so literally.

"How did you and your people come here, then?" he asked, and regretted it at once when he saw the look on her face.

"We were born here," she said. "Our ancestors brought their ships here several generations ago. It was our island. One day a terrible storm took it. We had never seen anything like it before. The rain was no rain at all—it rose from the sea and covered the trees like a cloak. The land tore apart and came back together. When it passed, it had changed. The mountains had grown, the rivers had split, the coves had reshaped. The stars were different."

James had navigated ships most of his life. He knew what that meant. "The island had moved?"

"Off the edges of the world," she said. "Our boats were gone, or smashed on the beach. We built new ones to fish, but every time we reach the horizon the waves rise up and push us back. They don't want us to leave."

"They?"

"The spirits," she said. "The fairies." Her face was still as stone. "They brought the island here for Peter."

"Peter?" His heart leaped. Beside him, he felt Gwendolen start. "Peter Pan?"

She nodded, just once. "We are all here because of him. The island was brought here because their child-king wanted a home. They brought us here because their child-king wanted an enemy to fight. They call us savages."

James squirmed inwardly. He didn't miss the look that Gwendolen shot him.

"How long ago was this?" A suspicion was rising in his head like a red dawn.

"Twenty winters, as near as we can tell," she said. "But time doesn't work the same here. The nights and days move according to the will of the spirits. We grow older, but slowly, as though something was doing its best to hold us back."

Twenty winters. The year that Peter had vanished from James's window, and come here. He had known Peter was going to Neverland; he hadn't questioned how this was possible, when he had made Neverland up. Fairies shouldn't exist—why not Neverland, if they were real after all?

But what if Neverland hadn't existed, until that night? What if the fairies had made it up too, more thoroughly and powerfully than he ever could?

"You spoke of others. You've seen others here, as well as Peter?"

"Many," she said. "The spirits bring them for Peter to play with. Always boys, though, and never as old as you."

He found he didn't like the sound of that. Where would they come from? Had they been flown out of orphanages and workhouses the way Peter had?

A dangerous place, Tiare had said.

Tiare was speaking again. "Now they've brought you here," she said. "I don't know what games you've been brought to play, but believe me, you're here to play them now. They won't let you leave either."

"Nobody brought us," James said firmly. He was glad the rest of the men weren't listening. They were spooked enough already. "I came by my own free will. I knew Peter when we were both young." She frowned, as if puzzled, but said nothing. "Do you know where I might find him?"

For the first time, she laughed—a harsh laugh, with no humour. "You haven't been listening, have you? If he wants you, he'll find you. There's nowhere you can go to escape him."

"Then surely it's best he not find me here?"

Her face stilled at that, and he knew he had struck a chord.

"Let me go to him. If you're correct, then wherever I walk our paths will cross. You don't need to be there when they do. And I can talk to him. Whatever he's doing to you, I'm sure I can make him stop—explain things to him."

"You can't *explain* things to Peter," Tiare said. "He visits us, at times—he isn't always our enemy. At times he even means well. But words roll off him like water hitting a rock."

That did, indeed, sound like Peter. "Surely it could do no harm to try?"

"No harm," she agreed. "And no good either." Her brows drew together, deep in thought. James waited, trying not to fidget, as respectful as he knew how to be.

"You may go," she said. "If you *do* have any influence over Peter Pan, then you're right that it should be tried. There is very little you could do to make things worse."

"Thank you." He tried not to let the full extent of his relief show on his face. "And my men?"

"They may stay here until you return," she said. "If they are respectful, they may stay as our guests. We will give them our protection."

"I'll talk to them. They will be respectful. You have my word as a gentleman." Neither of them needed to say out loud that the men would be more than guests. They would be

hostages, to ensure—what? James's return? His promise that he wouldn't return in the company of enemies?

It didn't matter. He had no intention of doing anything but what he promised, and it was a relief to have his men out of the way and out of trouble while he did it. Once he found Peter, this could all be set right.

GWENDOLEN AT least waited until they were outside the meeting house before she spoke.

"This is your paradise, is it?" she asked, as James had known she would.

"It's a misunderstanding. You heard me: I'll find Peter, and all will be well." He turned to face her. "You wait here with the men—see that they don't cause trouble. You know what they're like. I'll go alone. Peter knows me; it might not be safe for anybody else."

She laughed. "Forget that. I've been dragged this far; I'm not staying behind when we've finally arrived. Besides, if being around Peter isn't safe for anyone but you, then surely beside you is the safest place to be."

He didn't argue. He knew too well what it was like to stand back and watch someone else go to Neverland. Besides, he wanted to show her. Some deep-buried part of him still thought of Neverland as his own wonderful creation, and longed to show it off.

"Are you sure he *will* know you?" Gwendolen added. "For that matter, are you sure you'll know him? It's been a long time, James. You've both changed."

"We'll know each other." Her expression was still sceptical. He took her by the shoulders, willing his certainty to pass to her. "It's going to be all right now, Gwendolen. We're here now. We've made it."

"I'm still waiting to see where *here* is," she said.

NEVERLAND WAS bigger than it looked, which wasn't surprising. In James's stories, after all, it had always been exactly as big as it needed to be. This time, it needed to be big enough for a quest.

They headed inland, following the trickle of a stream into trees that grew thicker and stranger until they twisted like candelabra high overhead. James had never been near a wood when he had first told the stories, but this was a real wood, dense and green with gold specks dancing in shafts of sunlight. It was slow going through the roots and branches, and after a time they started to forget to be cautious and focus only on the path ahead.

It was a wondrous path. James and Gwendolen had visited many islands on their travels, including the uninhabited atolls that made up children's stories. They yielded surprising things, but they didn't have trees as high as the roof of a cathedral, trees whose vines shaped ladders that could be climbed and whose branches entwined into bridges that could be traversed. They didn't have huge skeletons of unknown creatures, weathered and made beautiful by time that couldn't have passed. They didn't have cave formations honeycombing the cliffs, all just waiting to be explored. They didn't smell of salt and moss and adventure.

It was dangerous, of course, as adventures needed to be. Even as careful as they were being, James started to lose concentration, and the next thing he knew his foot slipped on a scree of dirt and out over a deep gully. Gwendolen's hand grabbed at his elbow and snatched him back: the first time she had willingly touched him since the night he had killed their captain.

"Thank you," James said. His heart was hammering; the ache in his back had sharpened. Ever since that night, he had been terrified of another fall.

Gwendolen shrugged. "Couldn't have you snap your neck," she said. But she did it again the next time he stumbled, even though there was no cliff in sight at all.

As the sun started to burn hot through the trees they found a pool where one of the waterfalls fell, enveloped in a cool green glade. They had drunk at the village, but they hadn't been able to wash in fresh water for weeks. They did so now, plunging their heads beneath the clear surface, gasping and laughing at the shock of cold, splashing each other as though the tensions of the last few weeks had been washed away with the sweat and salt. As though the hard glint had never been in James's eyes, and Smithers had not died.

Gwendolen was straightening, combing her wet close-cropped hair back from her face, when James turned to her. His heart was hammering.

"Gwendolen..." he said, and when she turned he tilted her chin up, very gently, and kissed her. She hesitated for just

a moment—because the glint *had* been there, and Smithers *had* died, and they were a very long way from anywhere that made any sense—and then he felt her decide to kiss him back.

He remembered the first time they had lain together, three years after they had first run away to sea, the first time they could afford their own room in a shabby boarding house. He remembered their first kiss, a light, fluttering thing, questioning on her part and unsure on his. He remembered the way that kiss had deepened, taken root, grown into something wild and tender and urgent. He remembered lying with her afterwards, huddled under blankets as rain lashed the windows and rats scrabbled in the walls, trying to get used to the fact that he cared for another person again and that person was real and solid and curved against his shoulder in the dark. He remembered knowing he had left his childhood behind forever.

And yet here they were, in the midst of his childhood stories, trying to reclaim what he had never had.

"It *is* lovely here," Gwendolen said, as if against her will. "I do understand why you wanted to come."

It *was* lovely, it was true. But something was wrong. He had been trying to decide what it might be all morning; it came to him now. "I can't hear any birdsong," he said. "There were no fish in that pool either."

"Perhaps we scared them off," she suggested, but doubtfully.

"I don't think so." He struggled to put his feelings into words. "Neverland is meant to be filled with life. Apart from us, and the people in the village, have you seen any life at all? An insect, an animal, anything?"

"There was a vegetable patch at the village. And there are the trees. The whole island's full of those."

This was so undisputable that he thought for a moment his misgivings must have been wrong. And yet even the trees, now he was among them, didn't seem right. The leaves had a withered, autumnal look, though by his best calculations the island should have been in peak summer. When he had brushed against them climbing the mountain path, they fell in a cascade as if only lightly balanced on the branches. The entire island had the sepia fragility of a photograph.

"Perhaps," was all he said to Gwendolen. He sighed, and closed his eyes. Some of the burning obsession that had fuelled him since the appearance of the star had faded. Now the cold water was drying in the heat of the sun, his head felt filled with grit and his limbs were heavy. "Perhaps I'm imagining things. I'm tired."

"If you're right, this whole island is nothing but your imagination," she reminded him, then relented. "But I'm tired too. We could stop for a rest here."

He shook his head quickly. "No. Let's keep going."

His own reaction helped him place what else was troubling him—had been, in fact, since they had docked in the lagoon. He didn't want to stop. It wasn't only that he wanted to press on to find Peter. He didn't feel safe. This was his island, the place of his childhood stories. He should have felt the safest he had felt in weeks; it should have been the first chance he'd had to stretch out, close his aching eyes, and rest. He didn't dare.

This wasn't right. There was no fear in Neverland, and no death. And yet everything was dying, and he felt so very afraid.

THE SUN was almost below the horizon when at last they saw it. In the distance, a stir of movement. A shadow in the trees.

"Is that—?" Gwendolen began. James barely heard her. In that moment, she wasn't real to him. He knew that shadow.

"Peter!" he cried, as he had called from the rooftops all those years ago. His whole soul was in that cry. Back at the encampment, the crew heard it, and the hairs rose on the backs of their necks. "Peter, come back!"

His cry had gone unheeded when he was a child. This time, the shadow halted. It turned in mid-air. James held his breath, as a man does carrying a cup filled to the brim with water and fearful that a wrong movement will tip and spill.

The shape came back through the trees, and lit on the ground.

It was Peter.

V

The Home Under the Ground

It was Peter exactly as he had been on the night that James had last seen him: a young boy, fair and strong, with a tousle of curls and tiny feral teeth that gleamed in the twilight. The sun had bronzed his skin, the thin workhouse shirt had been replaced by skeleton leaves and tree sap, and sea-salt and stardust and summer wind had burned away any trace of London fog in his soul. But he hadn't grown.

Their child-king. Now James understood why the chieftain had looked so puzzled when he had said that he and Peter had been young together.

Peter hovered warily in mid-air, an impossible boy on an impossible island, and he and James stared at each other.

Peter, as usual, spoke first. "You're old," he said, with wonder.

"I'm not," James said, but it sounded weak to his own ears. "I'm younger than you—or I should be. Why are you still a child?"

Peter shrugged. "I didn't want to grow up."

"All children grow up."

"Except me. I told the fairies I wanted to always be a boy and have fun. So they stopped my heart."

It was then that James realised the only real change in Peter. The two of them were not far apart, and the night was quiet. But there was no faint, mysterious tick-tock. The clockwork in Peter's chest was silent.

"Peter," Gwendolen said, very carefully. James had almost forgotten she was there. Her face looking at Peter was surprisingly soft—as though, he caught himself thinking, she was talking to a child. "Where are the fairies now? Are they close?"

Peter shrugged. "I expect so. They're always about." He looked at her, head tilted to one side, and skimmed a little closer through the air. "What are you?"

She raised her head to meet him, defiant, as she had met James's eyes in the cabin after he had murdered his captain. It was only then James realised how unnerved she was. "I'm Gwendolen Darling."

"You look like my mother."

It startled James to hear it, because Gwendolen was still dressed as George, and nobody had ever thought George looked like a woman, much less a mother.

Gwendolen huffed a laugh. "I'm not your mother. Besides, I thought you ran away from her the day you were born?"

"I did," Peter agreed. "I went back once, though. That was when I saw her. I thought she'd have the window open for me,

but it was barred. She'd forgotten all about me, and there was another little boy sleeping in my bed."

"Really?" Her sympathy was tempered with evident scepticism. She had grown up in a workhouse. She knew how children made up stories. "Did you think to knock?"

"Why did you fly away from me?" James interrupted. He couldn't hold back any more. It was what he had come all the way across the world to ask. Peter glanced at him, with some surprise but little interest. "I needed you. You don't know what it was like in that place without you."

"I came here to have fun. The fairies made this place for me. It's my island."

"It isn't your island." James didn't realise he was raising his voice until he was shouting. "It's mine. You *stole* it!"

"James…" Gwendolen said, a note of warning in her voice.

He didn't care. In that instant, twenty years fell away from him. The shell of gentility that was Captain James Hook cracked, and what broke through was James, the orphan who never had anything except stories, and once a pan flute he had made. The flute he had given to Peter. But the stories were his. He had shared them only in the way one shares an embrace. He hadn't meant to lose them in the sharing.

Peter laughed, and the laugh held a trace of bewilderment. "I didn't steal from you, old man," he said. "I don't know you."

"What do you mean? Of course you know me. We grew up together."

"I didn't grow up." Peter's face hardened. "And I never saw you before in my life."

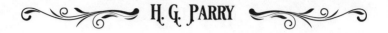

He meant it. The realisation was like a sword-thrust to the heart. Peter really had no idea who James was, or had ever been. His wonder had not been that James was grown up, as James had thought, but that there was a grown-up here in Neverland at all. He had no idea what the workhouse had been like for James after he had left, because he didn't remember being there. Peter never had remembered things for very long. He lived in the present.

And he was right. The boy he had betrayed no longer existed. Peter was still young, still innocent, still heartless. James was an old man, with a back that ached on cold nights and too many memories. Thirty-four. His mother had been so much younger than that when she died. This place was no longer for him. He could have cried, had he not been too old for tears.

As it was, he only stood there. Yet for some reason, Peter kept looking at him, head cocked to one side.

"Do you want to see my island?" he asked.

IT WAS the island James had spun out of words and dreams, on long cold nights. Peter explained it in a boastful, off-hand sort of way, and his explanations were half-remembered versions of the stories James had told him. The mountains where the Indians camped (he meant the islanders). The cove where mermaids sang (only there were no mermaids). The woods. The rivers. The caves where the Never bird nested (only there was no Never bird, either. There was nothing at all).

It was all James's island but for one thing, and that was Peter's hideout in the woods. Peter took them there last of all, too proud to see the recklessness in showing off a secret hiding place. It was dark by then—they had been walking all day, struggling to keep up with the small flitting form, and James was starving and exhausted, his feet blistered and his muscles sore. From Gwendolen's grim face, she was the same. Peter saw none of it. The glade was ringed by seven trees, each with a hole in the knotted wood small enough for a child to slip through.

"Those are doors," Peter said, with the boastful carelessness James remembered. It had seemed impressive at the time. Now he couldn't help but recognise a small boy bragging. "You're too big for them. But you can look through if you like."

"Why are there so many of them?" Gwendolen asked, out of breath.

Peter did a somersault in the air for glee. "You'll see."

Most of what James saw, craning his neck through the holes, was what he expected to see. He had invented Peter's hideout, after all. He knew the trees were hollow and opened to a single wide underground chamber carved out of earth and tree-roots, that there was a fire burning under a single chimney covered by a mushroom, that the room was otherwise dark but for the glints of treasure. He had not imagined the dank, musty smell as a child, but knew to expect it as an adult. What he hadn't expected was the hammocks suspended everywhere there was a space. Nor did he expect the

unmistakable shadows of others fast asleep within them. Small shadows, that turned and muttered with small voices as they dreamed.

A terrible chill took him. "Peter, are those children? Real children?"

"Those are the lost boys," Peter said proudly. "They're mine."

The spirits bring them for Peter to play with. Always boys, though, and never as old as you.

Dear god.

"Where do they come from?"

Peter shrugged carelessly. "I don't know," he said. "The fairies bring them. They talk about the streets at first. But they stop. Neverland makes them forget. What are streets?"

It seemed so much worse that Peter had forgotten the streets than that Peter had forgotten James. The streets were so much more real than James.

"How many of them?"

"They vary in numbers," Peter said. "As they get killed and so on."

The chill went to his stomach, and turned him sick. "What happens when they grow up?"

"They don't. You never grow up on this island. It's against the rules."

"But their hearts aren't like yours. They'll grow eventually."

"Oh, sometimes they do," Peter agreed. "But not all the way up. When they look to be getting a little old, I thin them out."

James didn't want to ask what that meant. Deep down, he knew.

"It's like the children's wing of the workhouse," Gwendolen said flatly.

"There's no work here," Peter said. "Well, not so's you'd notice. Do you want to meet them?" Before either of them could answer, he threw back his head and gave again the high, ululating crow.

They came pouring out of the trees, one through each door. Small boys, the youngest no more than three or four, the eldest perhaps eight or nine, all grubby and dirty and sharp-boned and long-haired. Their clothes hung in tatters on their skinny frames, and they carried makeshift weapons of sticks and stones. They had the look of half-grown puppies, all limbs and noise and desperate enthusiasm.

"Peter! Peter!"

The voices were achingly familiar, the west London twang that had once been James's own before he had forced it into a different shape and made it behave.

"Where have you been, Peter?"

"Is there any food for us?"

"Who's this?"

This last question might have applied to either of the two grown-ups, at both of whom they stared with undisguised curiosity, but Peter's gaze flickered to Gwendolen.

"I've brought her to you," Peter said proudly. "It's a mother."

"What does she do?" one of the boys cried.

Peter looked momentarily perplexed. "She tells stories."

"You haven't brought me anywhere!" Gwendolen snapped. She had recovered from the shock of the sleeping forms in the

hideout. Her jaw was clenched, and her hands balled into fists. "James did. He's the storyteller, not me. And I told you, I'm not your mother."

The boys ignored her. The smallest was now looking at James, puzzled. "Who's this one, then?"

Peter shrugged. "Can't remember. A pirate, I think."

This was greeted with a chorus of approval. "Can we fight him?"

"Will he fight *us*?"

"No!" James protested. "You're children. What sort of a pirate fights children?"

"A grown-up!" one of the boys declared, and the rest nodded in agreement.

James drew a deep breath, as Gwendolen always did, trying to find an anchor in a world that was spiralling away from him.

"I don't want to fight you," he said. "That's not why I'm here."

"Then why are you here?" the boy asked.

Because he had wanted to find Peter. That was the answer he had meant to give. But why had it not occurred to him, in all those years of longing for Peter, that Peter would no longer want him? It had happened, after all, to every other boy Peter had befriended. People were replaceable to Peter. They always had been.

James opened his mouth to answer the boy, to try to explain. Another voice answered first.

He came because we brought him here.

It was one voice, but it was also many voices. James turned, as did Gwendolen beside him, and came face to face with the light of a hundred tiny stars.

It was a swarm of fairies. Each one was very small, too small for human speech. Each could make only one chime at a time, like the one in the lantern on board the *White Bird*. But together, those chimes could entwine to make words, as individual notes entwine to make a symphony.

James Hook, they said. *We've been trying to find you for a long time.*

Gwendolen's mouth fell open in wonder. But James had stopped wondering at fairies on the night Peter had flown away. He had held one in his hand without a quiver of awe. They were a cold, scientific fact to him now, and he answered them accordingly. It never occurred to him that he had become a tragedy himself.

"What do you mean? *I* found *you*. And you didn't bring me here. I chased one of you across the world."

You could not have chased us, the fairies said, *had we not run.*

It couldn't be true. It couldn't be. He had searched for the island for most of his life. He couldn't bear to think that he had only succeeded because it had at last consented to be found.

And yet he had invented Neverland. He knew better than to think it could be found any other way.

"What do you want from me?" James asked.

The answer came in thousand chimes. *We need you for the reason they said. We need you to fight children.*

He shook his head, uncomprehending.

We need you to stay here. Peter Pan needs a villain to defeat. We need Captain Hook.

It was what he had come for, after all. He had wanted to run away to Neverland all his life; now he was here. He had wanted to be a pirate.

But not the villain. It was true that James Hook *had* been the villain at times, in the childhood stories, but that was before James had really understood what it meant. It was before he had learned about good form. (Although he supposed you could be a villain and still have that—a good many gentlemen seemed to manage it.) It was before he had met Gwendolen. It was before he had killed a man.

"Can't I—?" He stopped. He had meant to ask if he could be a lost boy instead but he knew already that he couldn't, and more importantly he didn't want to.

The fairies were still talking. *We need one other thing, as well. We need you to bring the island to life.*

That distracted him briefly from his own potential villainy. "Isn't it alive now?"

You saw it was not. You remarked upon it.

He flushed pink at the memory. Had they been watching him the entire time? Had they been listening?

It has what life we could give it. We made it for Peter long ago, when we took him back from the place where he was so unhappy. We made it as best we could. But we're very small, and only half real: barely more than belief and illusion ourselves. We couldn't do well enough. It's fading. Peter will live forever. Neverland needs to live with him.

"And what does that have to do with me?"

It needs you. You made it with words. You need to bring it life now with your heart's blood.

"How?" They didn't answer. "Will it hurt?"

Of course, they said.

"But if I do it, Neverland will live, and so will I? I'll be able to stay here?"

Oh yes, they said. *Forever.*

Gwendolen shifted beside him. "Don't do it, James."

"Why not?"

"Why not? Because this place is monstrous, that's why not! Look at these boys."

"They're better here than on the streets," James said, but it sounded unconvincing to his own ears. A lot of things, after all, were better than the streets. It didn't make them good.

"They're starving. They're filthy. And when they get too old, they're going to die. That's what Peter meant, wasn't it? He doesn't want them anymore, so he throws them away."

He couldn't deny it. "Perhaps the fairies can do something about that. Stop them growing."

"Don't you see what that would mean? No matter what happens, it will never get any better for them. How are things ever going to change if they can't grow?"

James looked at the boys, who were watching with a mixture of boredom and curiosity. They didn't find fairies very interesting, and certainly not when all they were doing was talking. He looked at their shabby clothes, their dirty hair, the many kinds of hunger that haunted their eyes. His heart

roared in his chest, as though it was trying to do not only its own work but that of Peter's which had stopped.

"If I stay here, and be your villain, and the island comes to life," James said to the fairies, "will you return these boys home, and stop stealing more?"

No, the fairies said. *Peter likes them.*

James looked at the island he had whispered into life in the dark. In the fading light the distant waves glittered, and the leaves overhead were as soft as a prayer.

"I'm sorry," he said. "I won't do it. Gwendolen's right. This place is monstrous."

It's Neverland, the fairies said. *Never work, never hurt, never fear. Never ending.*

"I know. It's not your fault; it's not Peter's fault. You only made what I told you to make. But I was a child. I didn't understand. You can't make a place without those things. And you can't make a place that never changes, never grows, never learns. That's not paradise. That's like Peter. That's a tragedy."

Then this place will be a tragedy, they said. *We don't care. As long as Peter is happy.*

"I know you don't care," James said. "But I'm sorry. I do."

He turned to Peter. His friend had lit on the ground beside him as the fairies talked. Standing, he seemed less unearthly—not the flying Peter Pan of James's stories, but the Peter who had slept beside James in the workhouse, fair and strong with enormous dark eyes in a child's face. It surprised James, though it shouldn't, to see that Peter was at barely the height of his chest. They had been so *young.* It had never occurred to him,

at the time or since, how young they had been. His throat tightened.

"I have to leave," he said. "I was wrong to come here."

Peter shrugged. It didn't matter to him what James did, as long as there was something else for him to do instead.

"You could come back with me." He said it on impulse, but once he had, it seemed so obvious. It was almost as though he had meant to bring Peter home all along. "You and the other boys. You don't have to stay here."

"This is my island," Peter said, but for the first time he sounded uncertain. "Where else should I be?"

"Anywhere you want to be."

"Well," Peter said, confident again, "I want to be here."

James knew better than to argue with Peter—it had never worked. The only way Peter ever agreed to anything was when it seemed to be his own idea. So he swallowed back his words, along with the lump in his throat.

"My ship is making berth at Skull Cove," he said instead. He tried to hold Peter's eyes with his own, which was difficult when Peter had taken flight once more. "It will be there until tomorrow. If you change your mind—if any of you do—I'll be there to take you away."

Peter ignored him completely this time. He flew in lazy circles above them, wider and wider, and James knew that when he turned to leave Peter would forget he existed at all.

"Goodbye," he said softly. He turned.

When Gwendolen moved to follow him, though, Peter's head snapped around in a flash.

"No," he said. His voice was different suddenly—low, imperious, the voice of a child used to getting his own way. It could have been ridiculous. It wasn't. "Not you. I told you, you're our mother."

As though at a command, two boys moved to block their path. They were small and frail, one dark-haired and one red-haired, both with thin faces and ragged clothes. They had no intention of moving.

"Don't be silly," James said. Behind them, he saw uneasily, the other boys had moved to block their retreat; two others had come in from the side. Wherever he looked, they were surrounded by Peter's children, enclosing them in a ring. And they weren't silly. In the shadows of the glade their faces were smooth and deadly and achingly young, brimming with a power that James had either never had or forgotten long ago.

"You can go," Peter said, from the air. "But leave her here."

"I'm not staying here!" Gwendolen said. "He dragged me into this in the first place. And *I* told *you*. I am not your mother."

The lost boys looked up at Peter. Peter nodded. It was all the warning James and Gwendolen had before the children converged upon them.

If the children had forgotten the streets as Peter had, they had not forgotten how to fight. Fists and feet rained down upon them, sharp and jagged and dirty. They grabbed at clothes and hair, they spit and kicked and punched and clawed.

Stop them, the fairies cried. *Don't let them leave.*

If their assailants had been bigger or stronger, James and Gwendolen might have fought them off. But these were *children*. James struggled, pushed, scratched with fingers and kicked with feet, yet when he made contact with the tiny, wiry bodies he couldn't help but hold back.

And so they were forced to the ground, still wriggling and lashing out under the weight of seven fierce, dirty street urchins.

VI

Do You Believe in Fairies?

JAMES and Gwendolen were too large to pass through the hollow trees, as Peter had said. So the lost boys built a house around them, a prison of thick branches and intertwined boughs. It took them until late into the night, and yet the children never complained. Their hands were calloused and blistered, and their wiry limbs were stronger than they looked.

"What do you mean to do with us?" James demanded of Peter. He tried to sound scornful, and Peter looked so infuriating turning lazy somersaults in the air and grinning that he almost managed it. "You can't keep us in here forever. For one thing, my men aren't far away."

"In the Indian encampment," Peter agreed. "I know. The fairies just told me. We'll attack them at dawn."

James cursed inwardly. "They're not Indian, you know," he said, out of sheer pedantry. "This is their island. You took it from them."

Peter shrugged. "Who cares?" he asked, which James had to admit was a fair question. He had been working on the seas his entire adult life, with the East India Company and on independent whaling vessels and everywhere in between, and nobody he had served under ever did care.

The fairies had gone long ago, bored by the long construction; the children left too, after being given empty bowls that Peter instructed them to pretend were filled with gruel. James and Gwendolen were left alone in their prison of ribbed branches, in the darkest part of the night. James twisted as best he could, grunting and swearing, until he could see Gwendolen's face. Most of it was in shadow, with only a faint glimmer of moonlight to highlight the edges of her sharp cheekbones.

"Are you all right?"

"No, James." She sounded both breathless and decidedly disgruntled. "I am not bloody all right. But I'm not hurt."

He was—at least, he ached all over, and he could feel the impact of sharp blows blossoming across his ribs and his shins. But she didn't ask, so he didn't say.

"I'm sorry," he said instead.

She laughed shortly. "What for?"

"All of it."

"All of it." She wasn't going to let him off that easy. "Killing Smithers, who never did a thing but try to help you? Dragging the ship off the edge of the world? Walking into the hands of tiny cutthroats?"

He closed his eyes. "Yes."

"Us, locked up in here at the fancy of a cruel, spoiled child? The men, about to be attacked at dawn? The village there about to be caught in the crossfire?"

"Yes! All of those things!"

The dream that he'd been walking in, the numbness that came from the hope of things soon getting better, fell away all at once. He remembered like the crash of an unexpected wave the look on Smithers's face as he had died, the fear and confusion of the crew, the long voyage through unknown waters so far from home. He remembered the darkest stories he had ever told about Neverland—stories about battles at dawn, about murders and scalping and the great monstrous crocodile that ate men alive, stories that had meant nothing to him as a child but were vivid and sharp and cruel now. He remembered that he was not a pirate.

"I'm sorry." Tears came to his eyes, hot and bitter. "I truly am. I'm sorry I made Neverland in the first place."

Her voice softened. "You can be hard on yourself for a lot of things," she said—dryly, but not unkindly. "Believe me. But not that. You were a child making up stories in the dark to get you through the next day. They were good stories, by the sounds of things. That's why I followed you here. I should have known better—I pretended I knew better—but I wanted them to be real too."

"Some of them were good. Others were brutal."

"That's the kind of stories children tell—they don't know any better. Of course they want to be pirates. Who wouldn't, if murder didn't mean anything?"

"I should have known better. I never knew what murder meant, not until Smithers. But I knew what death meant. I shouldn't have wished that on anybody."

"The people you killed in those stories weren't real," she said. "Only you and Peter were real. That's how it is for children playing games."

"It's not a game anymore."

"It is to Peter." She was silent for a moment, thinking. "I called him cruel just now, but he isn't really. There's something missing in him. None of this is real to him. I was watching when he gave those followers of his their bowls of imaginary gruel—it looked awful, when they were so hungry, but to him they were just as imaginary as the food, and it ought to satisfy them. He looks at you and sees a pirate because he wants to play pirates; he looks at me and sees a mother because he wants to play house."

This rang true, in ways he'd never been able to put into words before. But it wasn't the whole truth. "I think there's even more to it than that," he said cautiously. "He was always interested in mothers, from the moment I met him. It was one reason he craved stories, because he didn't have a mother to tell them to him. And the pirates—"

He broke off, because he could imagine Gwendolen's scepticism if he suggested that perhaps Peter wanted pirates because on some level they reminded him of James and the bond they had shared. That on some level he wanted a friend, but he could no more understand this of himself than he could understand that he wanted a mother. That he was *lonely*, in

a way that all the play in the world couldn't alleviate, and it would never get any better because he could never do anything else but play.

"Well," he amended. "Either way, we can't help him. I'm not a pirate. And you're nobody's mother."

"I am," she said, unexpectedly. She said it as matter-of-factly as she might correct him about the direction of the wind, or the likelihood of rain. "Or I will be. I'm carrying your child."

For a moment he sat very still, unable to move or breathe as the world remade itself around him.

"You might say something," she suggested, after the silence had gone on beyond polite limits.

James found his tongue, though it felt unfamiliar and strange. "Are you sure?"

"Am I sure I'm having a baby or am I sure it's yours?" She didn't wait for an answer. "Yes. I'm sure. I've been sure for a while now."

He scoured his memories for any hint, any sign of any such thing. There were none. If her body had changed, it had been hidden along with everything that marked her as a woman in the eyes of the crew. If she had been ill at any point crossing the Pacific, as he understood expectant mothers were, the weather had been rough and he had been too busy being ill himself to notice. She had been her usual self, strong and sure and dauntless.

"Only a few months," she amended, as if guessing his thoughts. "It's not going to happen anytime soon."

"But... Why didn't you tell me?"

"At first I wasn't sure what I wanted to do. Then I wasn't sure what *you* would want to do. I knew I had time to see out this voyage, and then I would have taken the profits from it and gone off to raise my child."

"As Gwendolen Darling?"

She misunderstood what he meant. "Well, I couldn't very well do it as George, could I? He'd have to be put away for a while. I'd miss him—I'd miss all of it—but that was always what this was about. Saving up enough to go and live my own life."

"No, I mean—alone? Unmarried? Without me?"

"*With* you, I hoped once." It was the first time her voice faltered. It made him realise that she hadn't been quite as matter-of-fact earlier as she'd sounded, and also that there *had* been a change in her lately. She'd been quieter, less certain, lost in thought at odd moments. She had been thinking about him. "But alone if you'd rather. This was never part of what we agreed. If you wanted to part ways, take your share of money, and get on with your life, you should just go."

There was no pause this time. He spoke as firmly and with as little thought as he had ever spoken in his life. "Never."

Nobody grows up, not really. There is no threshold to cross, no milestone to reach, no moment when a soul hardens from something malleable and uncertain to something fixed in stone. Everyone is always growing, all the time. But every so often there are moments when we stop, look back, and realise that we have grown without noticing, that we are no longer the same person we were before. James had felt it once when

he had lain beside Gwendolen in a rat-infested hovel, wondering at the unusual feeling of perfect happiness surging through his veins. He felt it again now, pressed beside her in a trap with their child a story waiting to be told between them. Peter's face came to his mind then, eternally young and heartless, and all he could think was what a tragedy he was.

They couldn't embrace, even if she had wanted to—and she didn't, not quite yet. There was still a lot to forgive. But their hands could reach each other, and she entwined her fingers around his and squeezed it tightly, in a way that felt like the start of an adventure.

"We're getting out of here," James said. "We're going home."

"We are." The pragmatism was back in her voice. "And we'd better do it fast, if we don't want these boys to kill our crew. You heard Peter—they attack at dawn. I wonder why dawn, anyway? Why not at night?"

"Bad form," James said, absently. "Peter and James never attacked except at dawn, in the stories." He didn't need to see Gwendolen's face to know she was looking at him like he was an idiot. "Do you think we can force this hut apart?"

"I think we could with someone helping from the outside."

"Who do you propose?"

"Peter," she said promptly. "It'll have to be him—the others are too scared to go against him."

"But he was the one who put us in here."

"You know him better than I do, James," she said, "but he didn't strike me as someone incapable of changing his mind. Am I right?"

"It's entirely possible that he's already forgotten he put us in here in the first place," James admitted. "But he won't forget to attack at dawn. He always loved war games. If you want to talk him into changing his mind, it'll have to be very soon. And we can't exactly go to him."

This time, he definitely saw the glitter of her wicked smile. "I might have that under control already."

IT DIDN'T take Peter long to come back. He burst from the tree like a shot from a cannon, face no longer laughing but red, contorted with fury. His tiny form hovered in front of James at eye level, vibrating, an angry wasp preparing to sting.

"*You* took it, didn't you? Filthy pirate!"

"He didn't," Gwendolen said, before James could ask what on earth Peter was on about. "I did."

It took her a bit of twisting, but she managed to whip it out from her belt with a flourish.

It was the flute. Peter's pan flute, the one that James had made for him all those years ago, scratched now and darkened with age but made of the same wood James had gathered in the workhouse. His jaw went slack.

"I lifted it while your boys were bringing us down." Gwendolen turned it in her fingers, deliberately provoking, her voice a smile. "You came just a little bit close. Confident men are always the easiest marks."

"I'm not a man!" Peter spat, furious. "I'm a boy! And I need that."

Gwendolen shrugged. "I'll give it to you if you let us go."

"Never!"

"Then you'll have to take it from us, won't you?" She tucked it into her hand and tossed her head. "It's a shame for you that you locked us up so tight. I can't think how you'll ever get to it."

James, belatedly, understood the plan. It wasn't to bargain for their release—that would be ideal, but Gwendolen must have seen that Peter was barely capable of bargaining. She was trying to provoke him into tearing apart the cage of boughs and coming in. He was strong enough to do it—James had no doubt of that. And once he did…

"I want my flute!"

"Come and get it then," Gwendolen shot back.

It might have worked like that. Peter was every bit angry enough to tear the hut apart with his bare hands; if they had thrown the pipe at him, it might have given them the chance to run. The lost boys would have chased them, but it was James's island as surely as it was Peter's. They might have got away.

But all at once, James didn't want it to be like that. Peter wasn't a wild animal to be tricked. He had been James's whole world once—he had been his friend. Here he was, more frightened and vulnerable than James had ever understood. This couldn't be how things ended between them.

"Peter," he said suddenly. "Do you remember Kensington Gardens?"

Most furious children, he had learned at the workhouse, could be startled out of a tantrum by a new idea. Peter was

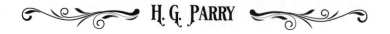

still white and seething, but he looked at him with a flicker of interest.

"You used to talk about it at the workhouse," James persisted. He knew Gwendolen would be looking at him as if, once again, he'd gone mad. "You said that you lived there for years and years, when you were a week old. You said you lived with the birds and the fairies, and played in the grounds after lock-up. I didn't believe you then."

"I never lived in any workhouse or Gardens," Peter said, but sullenly now. "I never lived anywhere but here. I ran away the day I was born. Give me my flute back."

"That's not true, Peter. I know why you say it, believe me." He was saying more now than he meant to say, more than he'd even realised he knew. "I tell everyone that my name is James Hook, and I went to Eton. I tell them I have a brother named George, and my father was a gentleman. But I'm a street urchin. If my father was a gentleman he seduced or raped my mother and abandoned her. I grew up in the workhouse. I grew up in the workhouse with Gwendolen, and with you."

"I didn't grow up!"

"No, that's true. But you were there while *I* grew up."

Peter shook his head mutinously.

"Then where did you get that flute? If you've been here your whole life, who gave it to you?"

"I don't remember. People give me things all the time."

"I gave it to you. I made it out of bits of old wood. It took me six months to carve it when you weren't looking, because I wanted you to have a birthday present."

"What's a birthday?"

"You say you ran away on the day you were born. Well, a birthday is the day you were born. Every year, on that day, you turn a year older. *You were turning twelve.*"

A shudder went through Peter, as though James had hit him.

"I made it for you," James repeated. "Because you were my friend. I don't know how you left Kensington Gardens, but you were raised in a foster home, and then brought to the workhouse when you were old enough. We met there. We were friends. I used to tell us both stories in the dark, when everyone else was asleep."

Something flickered in Peter's eyes. It wasn't a memory, not quite, but it was something good. "Stories."

"Yes. My name was James—it *is* James. I made up stories about Neverland, about Captain Hook. About you—about Peter Pan. Then the fairies came and took you away again, and they left me behind."

Peter drew closer, interested, the fury gone like a fire being doused. "Do you know more stories about me?"

"Yes." His fingers tightened around the wooden branches in a spasm of relief, the only sign he dared show. Peter never had been able to resist a story, and especially never one about himself. "Yes, I do. I'll tell you as many as you like. But Peter, you need to let us go, and you need to come with us."

"Why?" Peter didn't wait for an answer. "Are there more stories where you come from?"

"Yes." He thought of Portsmouth, the last time he had been there, the streets bustling with life, the shabby boarding house where he and Gwendolen had lain together while the rain pounded outside. The night their child had been conceived. "Yes, that's exactly what there are."

"Only I know all the ones here." James knew Peter's every mood, and never once had he heard him sound sad. But every so often there was a wistful quality to his voice. It was there now. "And none of the lost boys have ever been able to tell me any more."

"I'll tell you as many as you want. And what's more, you'll make more of your own."

Still Peter hesitated—wary, considering. James, acting on impulse, reached behind him and took the pan flute in his hand. He couldn't see Gwendolen's face, but he felt the reflexive tug of her fingers, and then she relinquished it.

"Here." He pushed it through a gap between the branches, willing Peter to come closer. "It's yours. We don't want to take from you. We—I want to help. I'm your friend, Peter. I always have been."

Peter still didn't remember him, James was certain of it. He didn't know what the workhouse was, or Kensington Gardens. The here and now was his island, and he had no interest in what lay over the seas. But perhaps something in him did, or perhaps it was simply that the allure of stories was engrained too deep to resist, because his fingers curled around the flute in James's hand.

"All right," Peter said, for all the world as though it meant nothing to him. "When do we go? Now?"

James could have wept with relief, or shouted his joy to the skies. Instead, he forced himself to slow down, to think, to

do nothing that might startle Peter out of his current mood. He knew from experience how easy that was to do.

"As soon as we can," he said. "But we have to be careful. The fairies won't want us to leave, I imagine. Are they watching us now?"

"Of course not." There was a touch of the old scorn in his voice. "They're asleep. They'll be awake during the day."

"Good. Then we have until daylight. Wake the others, and bring them to Skull Cove—quietly, mind." It felt like telling one of their childhood stories, alone in the dark. The words tumbled from him, and excitement rose in his chest. "We'll bring the crew; you can bring the other boys, and we'll meet on the *White Bird*. We can all go home together."

"The waves will push us back," Gwendolen reminded him—the first time she had spoken in a while.

"The fairies will be asleep, and the *White Bird* is a sound ship. I'll take my chances with the waves."

He meant it. In that moment, he was Captain James Hook. Nothing could stop him, and even death seemed an adventure.

The words seemed to have swept Peter up as well. He nodded, eager, as if James had proposed a new game.

"I can take the boat over the waves, anyway," he said.

"You can?" Gwendolen said, sceptical.

Peter nodded. "All it needs is some fairy dust. I'll pick it up and we'll fly all the way."

James knew better than to believe Peter could do everything he boasted of. But still, he remembered the glow around Peter as he had flown away, and his hopes rose, painful in their

buoyancy. Suppose it was true? Suppose they really could just fly away, as if they had never come? The lost boys rescued, the islanders left in peace, no harm done, except to Smithers, and he could spend the rest of his life atoning for that.

"That would be wonderful," he said, as calm as he could. "Thank you, Peter."

Peter grinned, the mischievous grin that at the workhouse had always meant trouble, and that James had always welcomed with his whole heart.

"I'll tell the others," he said.

James watched Peter glide away, his chest filled with something bittersweet and trembling, like tears or saltwater or light. This was it. This, after all, was what he had come to do. To be Peter's friend once more, in the world they had made together to keep the dark at bay. It wasn't until he felt Gwendolen's sharp elbow at his ribs that he realised the problem.

"Oh—Peter? Wait!"

The boy turned in mid-air, curious. James nodded to the thick branches crossing his vision. "You have to let us go first, remember?"

"Oh." Peter came back, and his small fingers curled around the branches. He tightened his grip, breathed in once, then threw them aside as though the deep-rooted boughs were nothing more than bits of driftwood in a child's sandfort. James flung his arm up instinctively to cover his face from the shower of dirt and twigs; when he lowered it, he was free. It was as simple and terrifying as that.

"Thank you," he said faintly.

Peter's chest puffed out with pride. "I'm very strong," he said. "Besides, the island likes me."

And then he was gone.

James clambered out of the hole in the wooden cage, his back screaming, his limbs cramping as they uncurled. He offered a hand to Gwendolen, but she ignored him, getting to her feet and brushing the dirt from her trousers. Her face was like stone.

"What's wrong?" he asked, knowing the answer.

"We had him," she said bluntly. "We could have been away. Now this is going to be a lot more dangerous."

"Surely you want to get those boys home?"

"Course I do—or I would, if I thought it were possible. I want to get the two of us home first. And Peter can't be trusted. You know that. All you've done is given him a new game to play. I thought you'd learned your lesson."

"If I haven't come to join them, then I need to have come to save them," he said. "I can't have come all this way, and done such terrible things, all for nothing."

"Oh," Gwendolen said flatly, "so it's about the story of James Hook."

He couldn't answer. "Whatever it's about, those boys need saving."

"A lot of people need saving. Doesn't make us the ones to save them." But she didn't have the heart to argue that point, and anyway it was too late now to stop, so she only gave him a hard look. "I won't forgive you again," she said. "You brought us here, and that's all right. You thought you were doing the

right thing. If you ruin our escape, then that's it. You'll never see me again."

"I understand," he said. He didn't say that if he ruined their escape, it was doubtful she'd ever have the chance.

VII
The Pirate Ship

THE men were difficult to wake. Only that morning, they had been at sea, fearful for their lives. They had celebrated their arrival by finishing off their ration of rum along with substantial quantities of the islanders' vegetable stores and dancing by the fire long into the night, and now they were happily curled up under the roof of the hut the islanders had provided. When James ordered them up, they merely groaned and burrowed deeper into their flax blankets.

James, by contrast, was trembling with exhaustion, feverish with excitement and fear. The journey back from Peter's tree had taken hours, hours in the dark along uphill paths and through trees that snatched at them with dying branches. It couldn't be long now until daylight.

"Get up, you bastards!" He had momentarily forgotten the language becoming to a gentleman. "Gwen—that is, George is at the ship. We don't have much time."

"Time for what?" Jukes blinked, in sleepy confusion. "I thought we'd got to where we wanted to be. Where are we going now?"

"London. Home."

"Where's that?"

It might have been only that they were half-drunk and drowsy. But James remembered, with a chill, what Peter had said of the lost boys. *Neverland makes them forget.*

Either way, it was too much to explain, even if there had been the time. "Am I not your captain?" he shouted, with all the breath left in his body. He kicked Mullins hard in the ribs, eliciting muffled swearing. "Move!"

Perhaps the red light had come once more into his eyes, or they had just woken all the way. Either way, they moved.

The islanders watched them go from their huts, silent and wary. James recovered himself enough to speak to Tiare, and thank her for her hospitality.

"We're taking Peter and the other boys," he said.

"That would be a good thing, if it were possible," she said. "They won't need us with their child-king gone."

"You could come with us," he offered.

"This is our island," she said. "We never wanted to leave. We want you to leave us alone."

This made perfect sense, and once again he felt a wash of shame. "I'm sorry," he said.

She didn't ask what he was sorry for, only nodded. "I hope you get away," she said. "For your sake, and for ours."

GWENDOLEN WAS at the helm of the *White Bird* when they arrived, puffing and sweating, at Skull Cove. Peter flew at her side, looking up at the masts. There was nobody else in sight.

"Where are the children?" James demanded. For a moment, he forgot that Peter was his long-lost, once-worshiped friend.

Peter shrugged. "What children?"

"He didn't bring them," Gwendolen answered tartly. "I can't get a straight answer out of him about it either. Sometimes he says they wanted to stay behind, other times he doesn't seem to remember they exist at all. I think he doesn't want to share this game with them."

"Bloody hell." James rubbed his aching temples, trying not to be annoyed. Peter couldn't help it. He had been made that way. "Well, we can't leave them."

"We'll have to." She didn't sound happy about it, but pragmatism always won out with Gwen. "The sun's nearly up. They'll be all right. The islanders will take them in, if Peter's gone and the fairies go with him. We can even come back for them. But for now we have to go."

She was right, and most of all about the sun. The sky was starting to lighten at the crease where it met the sea.

James made a decision. "Right. All aboard. We're leaving."

Incredibly, they had a fair breeze to take them away from shore, and the waves lapped gently at the ship. The sea was calm enough to reflect the last faint stars.

Second to the right and straight on till morning, James thought, a little wildly. His heart was pounding, and the air cooling the sweat on his skin was making him shiver. He wished the other lost boys had come.

"If you really can carry us, Peter," Gwendolen said dryly into the quiet, "now would be helpful."

"I told you," Peter said, from where he perched cross-legged on the prow of the ship like a figurehead taking a rest, "I'd need fairy dust. I'm strong, but I'm not *that* strong. I'd have to go get a fairy."

"Well, don't do that," James said quickly. Gwendolen didn't yet understand how literally Peter took things. "It won't hurt to take the slow path."

"You really *have* grown up," Gwendolen said, her eyebrows raised. "Or you've just gotten old."

James smiled, but he looked sideways to make sure Peter hadn't heard. He still wasn't convinced Peter had truly understood that leaving Neverland meant a chance of growing up—if not physically, for James wasn't sure if his clockwork heart could ever restart, then at least in other ways that mattered. A chance to learn things, for instance, without immediately forgetting them in the haze of Neverland. He might, perhaps, even remember James.

As long as they could get past the waves.

They had barely rounded the curve of the bay when a familiar cry went up from the starboard.

"Thar she blows!"

James's head whipped sharply in the direction of the call, puzzled. Skylights, almost falling over the side, leaned to point

out the movement in the distance. Something was certainly moving beneath the waves, something large. The water parted in front of it, as it would a whale very close to the surface.

But there was no whale. James saw it clearly the moment before it struck the prow: the flash of green scales, the glint of yellow teeth, the surging body.

"Hard to port!" he shouted, but the ship was already shuddering with the impact of a solid barrel of muscle. James fell forward, hard, and saw Gwendolen beside him do the same.

A crocodile.

James knew the crocodile all too well. It had been one of their favourite monsters—Peter Pan and Captain Hook had always lost many men to it, and James had described their losses in satisfying, bone-crunching detail. It was eight feet long, its mouth drawn back in a gaping grin, and it was unstoppable.

"What is it?" Peter asked, more interested than worried. He had let go of the prow at the impact, and was hovering at their side. His sword was drawn. Somehow that was less than comforting.

"If you don't know," Gwendolen said, breathless, "then how should we?"

"It was never here before!"

"The fairies must have made it," James said. He got to his feet with a grunt, wincing as his back throbbed. "They wanted to be sure we didn't escape. They took it from the stories."

"You and your bloody stories." Gwendolen had pulled herself up, and was scanning the horizon. "It's coming back around, look! There. Where are the harpoons?"

105

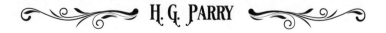

"Harpoons!" James bellowed, with all the force of years of practice.

His men had years of practice too. They may never have seen a crocodile before, but they knew how to kill a great beast at sea. Already the harpoons were being thrown overboard, each man pushing the other to take a shot at the writhing creature in the depths.

The crocodile twisted in the water, and the harpoons sailed past.

"Rifles!" Gwendolen shouted. "For God's sake, throw knives if you have to! Somebody kill it!"

It wasn't working. This was no great whale—it was smaller, faster, lithe and ferocious. Their harpoons were too bulky, and yet their rifles were too flimsy. The ship rocked under another blow from the creature's snout, and they all stumbled. There was a sickening crunch, and a splintering of wood.

"I think it took a bite that time," Peter remarked.

"Some use you are!" Gwendolen complained.

"Don't blame me!" Peter said, indignant. "It wouldn't hurt me, not if the fairies made it. It's him it wants."

He jerked his head at James.

James was about to protest, when in the light from the lanterns he saw Gwendolen's face. He knew its every mood, as well as he had once known Peter's. He knew the peculiar stillness it took when an idea had occurred to her, and the set of her jaw when she determined to act on it.

"Peter!" Gwendolen called. "When I give the word, throw me your sword."

"I don't take orders from anyone, pirate!" Peter retorted.

"You'll take orders from me! You said you wanted a mother, remember?" Surprisingly, Peter fell silent at this, considering. "James, keep still. Hold out your hand."

"What—?"

"I don't have time to explain. It's coming back around. Trust me."

But James understood already, and his heart quailed. It *was* him the crocodile wanted. The fairies had said as much—they needed Captain Hook, and for some reason they also needed his blood. The crocodile was here for both. It wouldn't hurt Peter; the rest of crew were nothing to it. It would come for him, wherever he went.

It would leave the water, and come on deck.

It would probably kill him before anyone could stop it, or at least hurt him almost to death. He knew that. But it was their only chance to destroy it, the only chance for Gwendolen and the crew to escape. The only chance to get Peter home.

James had never thought of himself as brave, not in real life. Captain James Hook was brave, or at least not wholly unheroic; the real James entered willingly into the dangers of life on sea, because he had to, but did everything he could to ensure his safety and that of his men. He wanted to live. And yet every story he had ever loved, even those of Peter Pan, had told him to give his own life to save those he loved. When it came to it, he didn't hesitate.

He braced himself on deck, pushed back the too-long curls he had modelled on an old picture of Charles II, and put out

his right hand. At his side, he felt Gwendolen take the other and squeeze it tightly.

"Come on, then!" he cried to the waves. "Let's see you, you filthy sea-dog!"

The crocodile came.

The weight of it as it clawed its way over the side pitched the ship almost flat; only years at sea in storms kept James firm on his feet. Its great bulk thrust across the deck at lightning speed, straight towards James. He heard as if from a distance his men diving below decks, saw the flash of teeth, and knew this was the end.

"Now!" Gwendolen snapped.

Peter soared from the top of the mainmast and threw his sword in a high, sweeping arc. At the same time, he dropped like a stone and landed in front of James. Right between him and the oncoming crocodile.

Peter had been right. The crocodile would never hurt him. It stopped short, jaws snapping closed, as though it had hit a brick wall. Its claws ground into the deck for purchase, scrabbling to avoid the small boy in front in it.

In the same moment, Gwendolen lunged on the monster and plunged her sword into its neck.

If it had been a real crocodile, it would not have worked. The blade was sharp, but slender; it would have broken like a twig on the thick scales and tough hide. But it had been made by the fairies, and as the fairies had told him, they weren't real enough themselves to make creatures of flesh and blood. This crocodile was mostly belief and illusion—out of

the water, the scales had a shimmering, liquid quality, and there were tiny gaps like ragged holes in blankets where imagination had failed. It was into one of these gaps that Gwendolen's sword stabbed.

The crocodile roared. Blood spattered from the wound—not red, but green and thick as tree sap. It thrashed wildly, its tail nearly sending Gwendolen flying, its claws scoring the deck. And then it simply vanished, as if it never was. The deck was slick with seawater, and nothing else.

Gwendolen laughed, half-triumphant, half-disbelieving. "It's gone! We did it!"

James pulled her towards him, and she wrapped her arms around him and kissed him as fiercely and joyfully as if there was no longer any reason not to. Her hat had fallen from her head, her eyes were shining, and she was George Hook and Gwendolen Darling both for all to see.

"You all right?" she said, briskly. "All in one piece?"

He had to pause to check, as though he were counting coins instead of arms and legs. "For now. Careful with that sword, though."

She grinned, and let him go, sword still in her hand.

"Come on, you cowards!" she yelled at the empty spaces where the crew had fled. "We still have the waves to get through!"

The men scrabbled from their hiding places, shamefaced and confused but too good a crew not to focus first on the sea.

And it was coming up fast. They now saw why the islanders, with their vastly superior seacraft, had not been able to leave. The *White Bird* had left Neverland in its wake; now

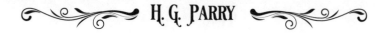

vast waves were crashing towards them, pushing them back even against the corresponding push of the wind. They rose high above the mast and crashed back down with the force of Neverland's own waterfall. James's spirits, which had risen, crashed down with them.

"My god," he whispered.

"Don't you dare give up now," Gwendolen said to him in a firm undertone, and raised her voice to the men. "Forward!"

The ship struggled forward.

The first wave pushed it back almost to shore; saltwater drowned the deck, soaking the few inches of James that weren't already drenched. He gasped with the cold and shock of it, then raised his head. It was nearly dawn. They hadn't fought a crocodile to be defeated by the ocean.

"Again!"

The second wave was more brutal than the first. The third spun them in a circle, nearly whisking James over the side, leaving him choking on a mouthful of spray and retching as his stomach heaved. Somewhere, he heard the shatter of glass.

"We're taking in water!" Jukes called from the wheel, and James remembered the flash of the crocodile's fangs and the terrible crunch at the prow of the ship. The waves plunged towards them, endless, undefeatable. James had been at sea his entire adult life. He knew they would never clear them. The waves would batter the ship to pieces, or push it back to shore. Back to Neverland, where the fairies would find them in the morning.

He looked at Gwendolen, saw her meet his eyes white and determined, and saw her nod sharply.

"Keep going!" he shouted back, because in that moment, as he had before he had jumped off a workhouse roof, he knew that he would rather die.

The ship juddered, rocked, swayed violently to one side. James cried out, and caught himself against the mainmast on reflex. At first all he could think was another crocodile had struck the side, or a wave had come from nowhere and nearly had them over. Then he heard Gwendolen gasp, and looked over the side.

They were flying.

The waves were receding beneath them—a few yards below, fifty, a hundred. They skimmed over them like a seabird, the sails rippling triumphantly in the breeze. James looked up, wondering, and saw Peter. His small, strong hands gripped the mast above James's head, and he lifted the ship as easily and lightly as he had torn apart the branches of the cage built for James and Gwendolen.

It was then that James noticed the shattered glass on the deck, and the faint shimmer of gold on the sails. He remembered, in amidst the chaos, the shatter of glass.

The fairy in the jar, the one who had led them here. They had forgotten about it, all the long day and night on shore. Peter had said that he needed only fairy dust, and the ship could fly.

"I didn't believe it," he said, out loud.

Peter looked down at him, face sparkling with mischief, and then turned to the sky with his eerie, ululating crow. James laughed out loud for pure delight.

"What's happened?" Gwendolen was looking at him, her face filled with wonder. "Is this it?"

"This is it," he said. "We're going home."

The ship was climbing higher and higher. The island was a tapestry in the distance—the smoke from the islanders' village rose from the clearing, and the trees were a dark blur over the mountains. The air about them was crisp and cold. The sky was tinted rosy pink now, and threaded with wisps of cloud.

"James," Peter said. The name startled him. The last time he had heard it in Peter's voice, they had been the same age.

James. James, give us a story. James, what about me? Who's Peter?

Goodbye, James.

"What is it?" he asked.

Peter's eyes were very dark and clear, like the sea in the Arctic. "I remember you. We're friends."

Joy, perfect and pure, rose like a bubble in James Hook's heart for the last time. It was as he had hoped. The mists of Neverland were clearing. His friend was coming back.

"Yes," he said. "We're friends."

A smile crossed Peter's face, softer than James had ever seen it. It was so fleeting that afterwards James was never sure if he'd seen it at all.

Then he frowned. "We were in the workhouse."

"Yes." Without quite knowing why, James felt a touch of foreboding. "We were. That's where we met."

"I hated it there. It was cold, and dark, and they made us work. And they were going to send me someplace. Someplace terrible. That's why I ran away."

"That's over with now." James glanced over at the prow of the ship, where Gwendolen stood braced. She was looking down at the waters far below, her face aglow with fairy dust, sword clenched in her right hand and her arm stained with the crocodile's green blood. "You're coming with us."

"But we're going back." Too late, James recognised the tone. In anyone else, he would have recognised it at once, but he had never heard it in Peter's voice before.

No. He had heard it once, and once only, the night that Peter had left.

Do you know what happens to the ones who fall between the cracks when winter comes?

Fear.

Peter hadn't run away because he had wanted adventure. James had always known that. He had run because he was afraid. He had wanted the stories because without them the dark scared him.

"Peter," James said, as calmly as he could. "It's all right. We're not going back to that. We got out, both of us."

"I got away," Peter said. His grip shifted on the mast, as if it was suddenly heavy.

No. Oh god, no.

"I got away," Peter repeated, "and now we're going back."

"Peter, listen to me." At the prow, his voice must have caught Gwendolen's ear. She turned towards him, curious, the fierce smile on her face slowly sharpening to worry. "Calm down."

"Get away from me!" It wasn't until then that James realised he had taken a step forward. Peter flinched away, and the

whole ship wobbled. Some of the men swore as they caught hold of the sides.

"You can't make me go back." There was no trace of joy in Peter's face now. It was all defiance, and beneath it, stark terror. "I can't go back. I can't."

"You don't have to." Even now, James couldn't believe it was happening. They had won. They were free. Only moments ago, there had been a smile on Peter's face, and he had spoken James's name. "We'll look after you. You can grow up with us."

"*I don't want to grow up*," Peter said, and he let go of the ship.

VIII
Hook or Me this Time

It was like falling from the roof of the workhouse all over again, only worse. So much worse.

Once again, he was plummeting, heart screaming, mind reeling, arms clawing on reflex for something, anything, knowing there was nothing to grab. Once again, there was cold air about him, and grey sky above him, and Peter was high above him flying away.

But this time he wasn't alone. All about him, the *White Bird* was falling too. He could hear the shrieks of his men, and the moaning of the great wooden masts. The crew's faces flashed before his own like terrible photographs. Jukes, clinging to the rigging, mouth contorted in a scream. Skylights, free-falling, spread-eagled across the sky.

Gwendolen.

She was looking towards him as the ship began to fall. There was just time, in the last second before the deck dropped

away from beneath their feet, for their eyes to meet; for James to see her face, sharp-boned and clever and entirely beloved, fall into lines of horror before she was whipped over the side of the ship like a piece of cloth in the wind.

"No!" James screamed, or thought he did, and then he hit the sea with the force of a cannon and his mouth filled with salt.

Nothing made sense. There was no up, no down, no light, no air. He was entangled in cloth, bubbles swirling about him, his lungs empty of breath. He thrashed and struggled and kicked on pure reflex, his mind filled only with Gwendolen. It wasn't too late. She had been alive the last time he had seen her. She was stronger than him, tougher, and a better swimmer. She always survived. If he could just *find* her—

Cold air hit his face as he broke the surface of the water. The ship was floating in a thousand pieces around him; the island was at his back; the waves were cresting and breaking towards the shore. He gasped, coughing helplessly, treading water.

"Gwendolen!" he called. There was no reply.

He searched the waves and the wreckage for what might have been hours, as the sky turned to grey and then to pale blue. He went under the water many times, resurfaced; he clung to barrels and bits of wood, scraping what was left of his strength back together and then striking out again. He found supplies, bits of the ship he recognised; once or twice he found the bodies of his men, shattered or drowned.

Peter was gone, vanished into the sky with the last of the stars.

There was no trace of Gwendolen. It was as if the sea had swallowed her up.

HE DIDN'T know how he came to be on shore. Perhaps the waves pushed him in, inch by struggling inch; he had a vague memory of seeing Gwendolen on the beach and thrashing towards her, though she vanished in a splash when he reached for her. All he knew was the feel of sand sucking at his legs where once there had been only sea, and that he was crying helplessly as he had not cried since his first night in the workhouse, terrible jagged sobs that would never stop.

It was over. Peter was gone. The lost boys would never be saved. The islanders were trapped in a bloodthirsty fantasy. Everyone that had sailed with him had died at his hand—Smithers murdered in hot blood, the rest of the men drowned following his orders. And Gwendolen—

Gwendolen.

Neverland had taken everything, and it was all his fault.

Neverland was all his fault.

The fairies found him there, when the sun was high in the sky.

You should not have tried to run, James Hook, they said in their thousand voices.

There were so many things he could have said to them—or could have screamed at them, because so much of this was their fault too. He only cared about one thing.

"Is she dead?" he asked.

Yes, they said. *She drowned. Her body is at the bottom of the sea.*

He had known, of course. But hearing it in such matter-of-fact terms cracked it open anew. His blood roared in his ears, and he sank to the ground. He almost didn't hear the fairies' next words.

We can bring her back, they said. *If that's what you want.*

"No," he said, uselessly, when the meaning had reached his ears. "Stop it. You can't. She's *dead*. You can't bring her back."

We brought Peter back.

"What do you mean you brought—?" The realisation momentarily quieted his grief. It still raged in his chest, but he raised his head, as if he had come up for air in the midst of drowning.

"He died, didn't he?" James said slowly. "Peter. He died when he was a week old."

We found him in the Gardens, the fairies said. *We don't know how he got there. Perhaps he ran away from home, or perhaps he fell from his perambulator like a bird from a nest. He was cold and wet and lonely. We tried to save him as he was, but his heart had broken. Our smith made him a new one from clockwork. We thought we were doing the right thing.*

"And you sent him to the workhouse?"

Not at first, they said. *We wanted him to live with us. He grew at first, but then we feared he would grow too big, so we stopped the clockwork in his heart. He stopped growing then. He lived with us for a long time.*

"He said he tried to go home," James said. Too late to matter, long puzzled-over pieces were fitting into place. "He said he tried to go home and the windows were barred against him."

He waited too long. He asked to go home, but when he saw his mother grieving for him he hesitated. By the time he changed his mind and went back, there was a new child in the nursery.

"But still," James said, "his mother would have known him. She would have taken him back."

His mother was dead. It wasn't her that he saw in the nursery that night. It was his younger sister, grown up, with a baby of her own. The fairies paused. *Things were different after that. We couldn't keep him happy. After a long time, we started his heart again, and sent him back to the human world. We left him on the doorstep of the house where his sister lived. But she couldn't have another child, and she didn't know who he was. She gave him away.*

She would have taken him to the Foundling Hospital, James assumed. He would have been fostered out to the country until he was older. Then he had found his way to the workhouse, like all the other poor and orphaned children. Like James himself. "But he wasn't happy there either."

The world was too cruel. He called on us to take him away. We couldn't bear it.

"And you couldn't take him back to the Gardens. You knew he wasn't happy there either."

No. The only place Peter was ever happy was in your stories. The only person he had ever wanted to be was Peter Pan. We stopped his heart again, so he could never grow up, and we made the stories for him to play in forever.

He could see it all so clearly now. They were fairies, after all. They couldn't be expected to understand that what had made Peter happy wasn't the story itself, but the *belonging*, the sense of a shared world that the two of them could enter whenever they chose. They didn't understand that stories weren't meant to be lived in forever; they were meant to be shared, passed on, questioned, to mingle with a thousand other tales and poems and experiences and be changed by them. They didn't understand that stories, too, needed to grow. He hadn't understood himself until recently. So they had taken Peter, and tried to fix him in a story as if in amber, and in doing so they had killed him all over again. James could understand it all, except for one thing.

"Why didn't you take me too?" he asked. "Why did you take him away from me, and leave me alone?"

We didn't realise then that Peter Pan needed a Captain Hook.

"But what about what *I* needed? I begged you take me. The world was too cruel for me too."

We didn't care about you. The answer came sweet and swift and brutal. *We only cared about Peter. We're very small, and feelings are very large. We can only care about one person at a time.*

"What about Gwendolen? Do you care at all about her?"

No, the fairies said. *But we will save her, if that is what it takes. If you agree to stay.*

Stay. It was what he had come to do, after all. He had come as Peter's friend, it was true, and they needed an enemy, but surely he could manage that. Peter had betrayed him. Because of him, his ship was at the bottom of the ocean, all

the men on it dead. Because of him Gwendolen was dead. His child would never be born. Surely he could hate Peter to the end of the world.

But it wasn't Peter's fault. He knew that, too clearly. Peter was a child—the purest form of a child that had ever existed, a child that would never grow to be anything else. His moods were quick, deep, fleeting things. He didn't understand the damage they could do. James was far too grown-up now to swear eternal vengeance on a frightened child. It would do him no good if he did, anyway. This was Peter's story. He would always win.

James looked out at the surface of the sea. It was brilliant blue, as he'd always imagined it as a child, and in the sun it looked very cold.

We have the whole ocean, Gwendolen had said, as they had chased a star across the world. It was what she had wanted as a child—to be free, unbound, to see the entire world. He hadn't listened. He didn't care about the ocean. And now the ocean had her.

"Save her." James looked back at the shimmer in the air. "If you do that, I'll be anybody you want me to be. I'll stay here forever, and I'll hunt Peter as much as he wants, and fight with him, and lose over and over again. I deserve it. Just let her go."

There's one more thing, they said. *We want your right hand.*

He thought he had been prepared for anything now, but of course he hadn't. His left hand crept to encircle his right wrist.

"But why? What do you want with it?"

We told you. We need you to give the island life.

"I gave it my life," James said, with all the bitterness he could muster. "I poured everything into this place, when I was a child."

You poured your words. Neverland needs more than your words if it is to survive. It needs your flesh and blood and bone.

And James knew this. He had always known this. Why else, right from the start, had the feared pirate Captain Hook been created without a hand? Magic required sacrifice. The version of himself he had created, the version that could live in Neverland, had been already mutilated.

Peter could only be what he was because the fairies had taken his heart. Nobody cared for James's heart: only Gwendolen, and she was dead.

"Save her," he said, "and you can have my hand. You can have my enmity. You can have all of me."

We want nothing else of you, James Hook, the fairies said.

The cut came from nowhere, as though the air itself was alive with thin blades. The blood came next, then the pain. James screamed, and doubled over. He snatched back the mutilated stump and cradled it to his chest, which didn't matter because the fairies had no further use for his arm. His imaginary island swam in front of his eyes, and he twisted in a ball of pain.

As he did so, the fairies took the hand that had once belonged to James, and threw it into the sea.

The hand arced through the sky. James saw it, half-dazed, the world grown soft and hazy beneath him as blood pulsed. It seemed to take its time, a slow leisurely climb and descent.

Time enough for one last story.

It was all he had been able to think to do, and now he wasn't sure if he could do it. Gasping, with what he thought must be the absolute last of his strength, James summoned that story to his heart. He gave it everything he had left, all the years that passed between the child telling Peter Pan about Neverland in the dark and the pirate who had murdered his captain and brought his crew to its shores. He gave it everything that had ever passed between him and Gwendolen, her fierceness and their love and his failure. He threw that story after his right hand. It landed just as the hand hit the waves.

The ocean convulsed. The island shivered. Around them, the fading trees creaked; leaves grew on the bare branches. Bird-song crept into the trees, and voices whispered on the wind. There was a pirate ship in the lagoon, and a plume of smoke in the mountain. Flowers blossomed the colour of blood.

It is done, said the fairies. *The stories may begin.*

Neverland had been born.

James saw nothing of this. Shuddering, sobbing, he had just the presence of mind left to rip off his neckerchief and clumsily wrap his wrist. It was difficult, with his left hand and with the throbbing faintness behind his eyes.

He had thought, when he had made the bargain, that he would feel nothing over the agony in his heart. But it hurts very much to lose a hand.

"What about Gwen?" he managed. "Where is she? You promised—"

We keep our promises. There is your wife, James Hook.

James followed the tiny pointed finger. It led out to sea, where the waves danced.

We would have made her a mother for Peter, the fairies said. *But she needed more than a new heart. Her body had drowned. It was filled with water. She needed a new one, one that could breathe it in. But we have made one of those before. We knew what to do. She lives.*

The waves crested and broke. He saw her.

She was eight feet long, sinuous, and scaled. Water poured from her back, and streamed from the sharp line of her tail. Her mouth was turned up at the corners in an eternal, sharp-toothed crocodile smile.

They hadn't needed to tell him about her heart. He could hear, even over the sea and his own heart finally breaking, the loud, ominous tick-tock.

IX

The Return Home

There are only few more things that need telling.

❦

NEVERLAND, EVENING.

James had lain in the mud a long time, shivering and sobbing, agony radiating from the stump of his arm and the world around him receding like the stars on the clearest Arctic nights. The scent of blood and salt filled his lungs, his stomach roiled, and vast swathes of time passed him by without leaving a mark. He knew he couldn't survive, and he was glad of it. And yet, as he had found so many years ago when he had fallen from the workhouse roof, it is very hard to die of pain and misery alone. If your injuries don't kill you, sooner or later you have to get up.

James got up in the evening of the second day, as the sky softened to deep blue and the Never bird piped its song

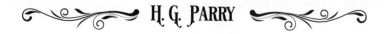

through the trees. He was weak and dizzy, and desperately thirsty—what drove him at last to movement was the splashing of mermaids in the lagoon not far distant and the dry rasp of his own throat in response. Fortunately, there was a trickle of a stream close by, doubtless flowing down from the pool where he and Gwendolen had bathed. He drank deeply, rested a little longer, then rose to his feet.

He thought he had nowhere to go, and nobody to find. He had forgotten the second part of his promise—his promise to be Captain Hook. He had not gone far along the path to Skull Cove when he heard the sound of rough voices raised in song, the beat of boots on the deck of a ship, the jaunty chirp of a harmonica. The *White Bird* floated in the harbour as though it never been beneath the waves, except that its name had been erased from the hull and the flag flew the gaping grin of the Jolly Roger. Captain Hook's ship was ready for him.

Captain Hook's men were still aboard.

Not James's men, of course: those were lost to the bottom of the ocean. These were his pirates, the rag-tag crew of scoundrels and ruffians dreamed into being by his childhood stories. But they bore the faces of his old crew, the crew of the *White Bird* who had followed him across the world. Jukes. Cookson. Starkey. Mason. Mullins. Skylights, who had been the cabin boy. And one other, another face that he couldn't quite recognise, except as the face of somebody who was dead.

It was difficult to remember things in Neverland. It was made of stories, and it was the job of stories to make their

listeners forget everything but the story they were being told. Mere hours ago, the face of Captain Patrick Smithers had been etched on James's brain in acid. He had remembered the look in his eyes as he had died. He had known that the *White Bird* had no first mate, because he himself had been first mate, until he had murdered his captain and taken command. Now, Captain Hook had killed so many people they had grown hazy, and certainly he had always been in command. He saw only his bo'sun, waiting for him.

"It's me," Smithers said, but James misheard, or pretended to. His mind was already forgetting how to tell the difference.

"So it is, Smee," he said, and stepped on board his ship.

NEVERLAND, IN the early morning.

Captain Hook had set out for a morning constitutional, something he felt vaguely was good form, the sort of thing that had been encouraged in his boyhood at Eton. The trees had grown strong and thick of late. He followed the shoreline of the lagoon, picking his way over the sturdier tree roots, cutting the occasional stray branch out of his way with the hook on his right arm. He was used to the hook now. On the whole, he preferred it to his hand, it being far more practical for combing the hair and other homely uses. If he was a mother, he often said, he would pray to have his children born with one. But it did hurt sometimes. So did the twinge deep inside him when he spoke of mothers and children, as though at something he couldn't quite forget.

It had been six months since Neverland had been born. In most respects, this made no difference to the pirates. There was no real weather in Neverland—the sky never changed, except at the whim of Peter; there was no risk of frost or drought or storms. The island's inhabitants experienced time, as Peter did not; the indigenous village still grew their crops and hunted and reared animals for meat. But all the pirates did was plunder, and that was not seasonal work. There was only one reason James should have been counting the unfolding weeks, and he hadn't remembered what it was.

He was on the other side of the lagoon, his ship distant and small as a model in a bath, when the ground before him burst apart. The Never bird took flight in front of him, a flurry of yellow and red and gold rising from the ground like a pantomime ghost. James leapt back, slipping in the mud, spluttering.

"Brimstone and gall!" he snapped, which was the way that Captain Hook cursed. He would have gone on, but something stopped him short.

The Never bird had dislodged a flurry of leaves as it had left, leaving exposed a hollow nest made of twigs and mud and soft feathers. There in the nest was a single egg, the largest James had ever seen, so large that he knew at once it didn't belong to the Never bird. Even as James crouched down beside it, wondering, the papery shell began to crack and then to fall apart.

Inside the eggshell was a baby, a newborn, pink and round with a head full of black curls and black eyebrows that were already the mirror of James's own. It stared up at James, blue

eyes round and wondering and unfocused, and gave a very soft chirp. All James could think, at first, was that Peter had once told him that all children had once been birds.

This egg didn't come from any bird, though. When James took up the child in shaking arms, careful not to scratch the soft skin with the hook that all at once seemed barbed and cruel, a flash out in the water caught his eye. He turned, just in time to see a shining tail disappear beneath the waves, and then the shimmer of a sinuous body going down to the depths. If he listened carefully, he knew, he would hear the clockwork sound of Gwendolen's new heart.

He remembered.

"Thank you," he said, too quietly to be heard, knowing he would be heard anyway. "I won't fail you."

He didn't dare return to the pirate ship. Once there, he would be nothing but Captain Hook. He wouldn't know who the child in his arms was, or why he had brought it home; he would throw it overboard, or give it to Smee to train as a cabin boy, or leave it in the woods for Peter to find. Trying to hold on to his thoughts, his memories, these days was like trying to catch smoke. Often he went whole days without remembering where he had come from, or why he was so sad. Usually he was glad of it. But this time, perhaps for the last time, he needed to be James again.

Even in the woods it was difficult. He had a notebook and pencil in his pocket, because Captain Hook fancied himself an amateur botanist. But it was difficult to write the letter; more difficult still to pick up the infant in his one

good arm, wrap him warmly in his scarlet coat, and take him to the glittering caverns where the rocks would echo his voice.

"Peter!" he called. "I know you can hear me."

There was no response. And yet James had a suspicion that he was right nonetheless—he suspected, in fact, that Peter was close by him more often than his childhood friend let on. They had fought many battles already, of course, without a trace of recognition on Peter's part and often none on James's. They played their parts in the stories, all blood and steel and adventures, and that was it. But here, in the place between the stories, perhaps things were different.

"Peter," he said. "I have a boy here."

No reply. He persevered.

"This boy's name is George Darling. I need you to take him to London, to the Foundling Hospital. I need you to take him with this letter, that will give them his name and his mother's."

He waited, ears straining. There was no reply.

"Please," he said. "Please don't let him grow up here."

Nothing.

Not even an echo.

And then…

"Why should I?" Peter's voice echoed.

James fought to keep the gush of relief out of his own voice. He had not been sure, after all, that Peter would come.

"Because it was our fault," he said, "and we need to put right what we can. Because Gwendolen wanted it. Because we

were friends once, a long time ago, when we were very young." None of this meant anything to Peter, of course. "Because it would be an adventure."

The silence that greeted this felt different, hesitant, attracted.

"You're not *afraid*, are you, boy?" James said, in his most contemptuous sneer.

That did it. There was a rush of wind, a wind that smelled of autumn leaves and clear skies and adventure, and then Peter was before him. His face, so wild and so young, was defiant.

"Give him to me, old man," Peter said.

"Will you swear to take him to the Foundling Hospital and nowhere else?"

"I swear," Peter said, so grandly that James knew it stood a chance of being true. Peter had no honour, but he did have more than the usual serving of pride.

Baby George had fallen asleep in the crook of James's arm, and seemed to have doubled in weight and warmth in the process, like a small burning star generating his own gravity. He made a mewling noise as James shifted him, and nestled deeper into the folds of James's pirate coat. James kissed the boy very gently on his fuzzy head, telling himself that he wasn't trembling, his eyes weren't burning, that he wouldn't even remember the boy by the morning. Only the last, in fact, was true.

His heart cried, *no, no*, as he handed the child to Peter, but his heart had broken long ago and its voice was very faint. He barely heard it.

"Don't let her down," he said to Peter. It was a foolish thing to say, he knew. Peter had no idea who Gwendolen was, and no heart at all.

And yet…

"Never," Peter said, as though he had both.

It was a pretend, of course. But Peter took pretends very seriously.

James watched Peter soar into the sky with his only child. He would never see George Darling again.

NIGHTFALL OVER Neverland.

Captain James Hook lay in the stateroom aboard his ship. On the deck above his head, he heard the thump of booted feet, and the call of cheerful voices. His pirates were always cheerful, always bloodthirsty, always ready for action. It was exhausting. That day he had grown so frustrated with their caricatured enthusiasm that the red light had kindled in his eyes, the last of James had gone away in a wash of pounding blood, and when he came back again Skylights was dead at his feet. It didn't bother the other pirates one bit. By sunset they had forgotten there had ever been a Skylights, and so for the most part had James. It was possible that by tomorrow Skylights might even be back at his usual place at the breakfast table, death forgotten along with everything else.

To die would be an awfully big adventure.

James felt a bump on the foot of his bed, and then heard a voice.

"Why are you crying?"

It was as low and as quiet as it had been in a different darkness, a world away.

James should have snatched for his pistol or his sword at once. It was his role, after all, and what was more most of the time these days he wanted to. But his pistol was out of shot, and his sword was out of reach. Besides, he was tired. The stump of his right arm throbbed dully in its iron hook.

"Who are you?" James asked the darkness. "Do you even remember?"

"I am youth," Peter said. He was just saying things, as usual. "I am joy. Why are you crying?"

James shook his head. "You wouldn't understand."

Peter didn't argue. It was true. He was youth and joy. He was innocent and heartless. He couldn't even understand tears, much less the feelings that lay beyond them.

"I took the baby to that place," Peter said, after a while.

It startled James; for the first time he turned to look at Peter properly. But he couldn't see him in the dark. "Good," he said. "Thank you."

He wished there had been somewhere better than the Foundling Hospital for Gwendolen's child, where it was all too likely that the boy would end up in a workhouse as he and Peter had done. But he would be fostered in the country first, and taken care of. The letter had given him a name, and there had been enough pirate treasure in the pocket of his coat to give the boy an inheritance when he came of age, assuming it fell into honest hands. Perhaps George Darling would be one of the lucky ones, adopted by a good family. At least he would have the chance.

"I'll keep a watch on him," Peter said, as if he read James's mind.

"Don't touch him," James warned.

"I won't," Peter said carelessly. "I have enough boys, and he was too young."

"He'll grow up."

"I know." A shudder, exaggerated, like a child encountering a hated vegetable. "He'll grow all the way up. He'll become a man, and work in an office, and get married, and find a mother for children of his own."

Another tragedy, or perhaps a mercy: that Peter had convinced himself that was the worst that growing up had to offer. "Don't touch her either."

"I won't. She'll be too old. If there's ever a little girl, I might take her."

He should protest that, he knew. Gwendolen's son deserved to grow up away from all this, and so did their children and their children's children. But Peter wouldn't listen to his protests, or remember them if he did. And perhaps something in him weakened at the thought of a young girl, another Gwendolen Darling, looking at him as Gwendolen had looked in the darkness of the workhouse night the first time he ever saw her. He probably wouldn't recognise her by then, or know her as his own grandchild as well as Gwendolen's. But the selfish part of him wanted to see her anyway.

Perhaps, after all, she would be the one to end it.

"James?" The name startled him, as did Peter's voice, unexpectedly quiet. He remembered hearing that voice in the dark a lifetime ago in another world, soft and defenceless as a crab that had lost its shell. He felt the bunk shift as Peter settled at his feet. "Tell us a story."

"I don't have any stories left," James said. "I gave you all of them long ago, when I was too young to realise how dangerous they could be, and then I tried to take them back when I should have known better. I gave my last one when the fairies chopped off my hand to feed the island. The very last of James Hook went into that. Anything left is just an echo, like the ones at Skull Cove, getting weaker and weaker all the time."

"What was that story?"

"Never mind."

Peter was quiet, quiet enough that had they been back at the workhouse lying side by side in the dark James would have been able to hear the tick of his heart. The last time he had heard that sound had been Peter's last night in the workhouse, before he had flown away for good. He had wrapped James in an embrace, the first and last time he had ever done such a thing, and the clockwork had fluttered between them as Peter had whispered goodbye.

Of all the things James could never forgive Peter, that embrace was the worst. Without it, he might have been willing to let the story end there. Without it, he would never have known that Peter loved him, and always would, even if he never remembered it again. Without it, he could have hated him.

"Another one then," Peter said. "Please."

James sighed. "One last story," he said. "One day, the creature that used to be Gwendolen will kill me. She'll follow me, ticking away the hours of my life. I should turn and meet her. I deserve my death. But no matter how I try, I will never be able to face looking her in the eyes. So I'll always turn and run, and she'll pursue me wherever I go. After a while I won't even know why. I daresay the island will make something up."

"That's not a very good story," Peter said uncertainly.

"That's not the story," James said. "The story is this. One day, you'll come to fight me. Perhaps I'll take something of yours, as Gwendolen took those pipes, and you'll try to take it back. You'll come to fight me, and you'll win. You'll deliver me to Gwen. And that will be an end to it."

"Nothing ends in Neverland," Peter said, but his fingers curled around the pipes at his belt. "No work, no pain, no endings."

"I will," James said. "That's my last act of story. I will work. I will hurt. And I will end."

Peter considered this as well as he could. "But not me," he said. "I won't end."

"No," James said. "No, there will always be stories of you."

"Good," Peter said. "The dark's too big without them."

THERE WILL always be stories of Peter Pan. The fairies saw to that when they brought the island to life with James's blood and brains, when the water frothed and boiled and a

childhood's worth of night-time imaginings teemed from his head. Adventures of pirates and battles, poisoned cakes and Never birds, fairies and lions and wolves and grizzly bears and mermaids. So many stories poured into the island that day that they never noticed the very last one of all, the thread that runs through the fabric of the island, the pulse that beats beneath every gilded adventure.

This is the story James told as Neverland cut his hand from him and cast it into the waves, the story written in his own heart's-blood.

The children grow up.

They come to Neverland one by one, stolen from their beds by fairies or dreams or Peter himself. They have all the adventures they could want, golden days and starlit nights of them, brimming with the danger and cruelty and bloodshed of childhood imagination. They have so much fun that they almost forget the world they came from.

But they don't forget, not entirely. The hand that wrote Neverland was no longer a child's hand. It was a grown-up hand, pumping with the blood of a grown-up heart, a heart whose owner knew loss and guilt and love. Those things are now written into Neverland too.

So the children don't quite forget either. Even as they play, they remember there are others out there in the world, and they know without quite understanding that they are loved and missed and mourned. The longer they stay in Neverland, the more they are troubled by the feelings of those they've left behind. The world around them starts to seem not quite

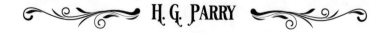

real. They start to wonder if there are better, richer stories out there, waiting to be found.

One night, they conquer all the demons Neverland has to offer, and leave the island as they might wake from a dream. They go back through the nursery window to their beds, and the next morning they begin, day by day, to grow up. They find that growing doesn't need to mean losing, and doesn't need to mean growing into what anyone wants them to be. They still have Neverland running through their veins like the echoes of a fever, but they find other stories too, as many as they could possibly want, and all those stories mingle to make them the person they are. They have the whole ocean, every country, and every last bit of sky. They fall in love and have children of their own, or they don't. They grow so much that they learn to smile and cry at the same time.

Let them.

Let them write their own stories.

Let all children, except one, grow up.

Thus perished James Hook.

> *[Peter] had one of his dreams that night, and cried*
> *in his sleep for a long time, and Wendy held him tight.*
> —*Peter Pan*, Chapter 15, "Hook or Me This Time"

Acknowledgements

Thank you to my agent, Hannah Bowman, and to the amazing crew at Subterranean Press: Bill Schafer, for asking for this story in the first place and giving it such an amazing home; Navah Wolfe, for her insightful and generous editorial comments; Geralyn Lance, production manager; and Shannon Page and Allison Young, for copy edits. Eternal thanks to Kathleen Jennings for her incredible artwork and design—it's such a privilege to have it on my cover.

Thanks, as always, to my family: to my Mum and Dad, to my sister, and to the houseful of small creatures who helped by being no help at all. Special thanks to my sister Sarah, who came up with the idea of James and Peter knowing each other as children and yet was so kind about letting me fly off with it.

And, of course, thank you to J. M. Barrie, for creating the strange, twisted masterpieces that are *Peter Pan*, *Peter Pan in Kensington Gardens*, and *Peter and Wendy*. The dark would be so much bigger without them.

About the Author

H. G. Parry is the author of *The Unlikely Escape of Uriah Heep*, the *Shadow Histories* duology, and *The Magician's Daughter*. She holds a PhD in English Literature from Victoria University of Wellington, and currently lives in a book-infested flat on the Kāpiti Coast in New Zealand, which she shares with her sister and an increasing menagerie of small animals.